# Deadly Collection

## Jeffrey B. Martin Jr.

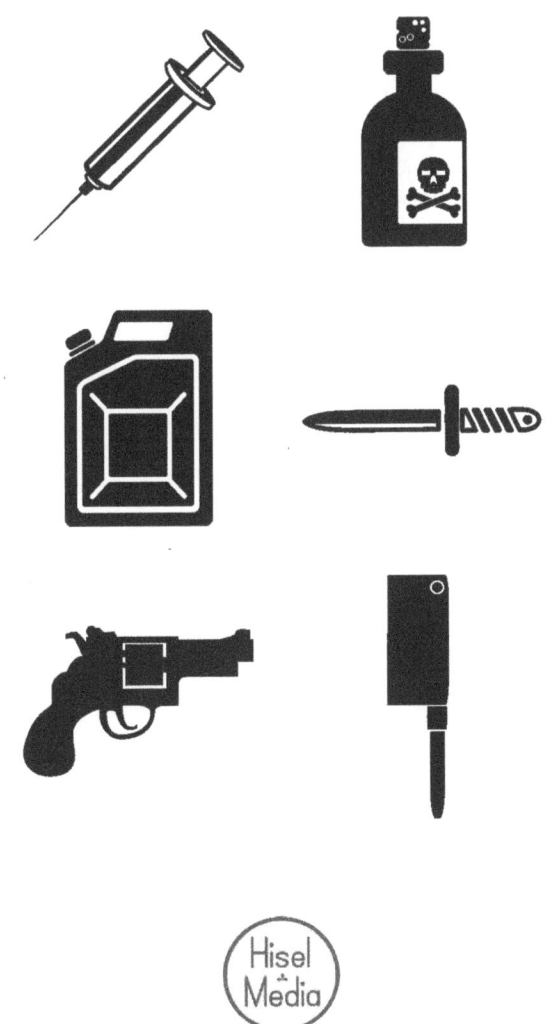

**This book is a work of fiction.** Names, places, characters, and incidents either are products of the author's imagination or are used fictitiously. Any resemblance to actual persons, living or deceased, events, or locales is entirely coincidental.

**All rights reserved.** No part of this publication may be reproduced, distributed, stored in a database or retrieval system, or transmitted in any form or by any means—by electronic, mechanical, photocopying, recording, or otherwise—without prior written permission from Hisel Media. For permissions, contact Hisel Media at the address listed below.

### Rightsholder and Copyrights
Exclusive worldwide print and electronic publishing, distribution, sales, and licensing rights held by Hisel Media.

Literary work © Jeffrey B. Martin Jr.
Cover design © D.M. Gaynes

### Contributors
Author: Jeffrey B. Martin Jr.
Publisher: Hisel Media
Acquisitions editor: Cheryll Franco
Copy editor: Rob Montaigne
Cover and interior design: D.M. Gaynes

### Charity
A portion of the proceeds of this book go to Intrepid Fallen Heroes Fund.

### Contact Publisher
Hisel Media
P.O. Box 6716
Malibu, CA 90264

### Ordering Information
For wholesale orders or high quantity discounts, contact Hisel Media at the address above or at sales@hiselmedia.com.

First printing: 2017

ISBN: 978-1-63301-007-9

# Prologue

Dr. Lucas Calling,
    We have determined that your medical practices are too much of a liability for Bourne Hospital. This organization cannot risk further litigation over your treatment protocols. Therefore we are terminating your employment, effective immediately. The board members have decided to offer you a fair severance package for the commitment and perseverance that you have shown in the past. You can file an appeal with the administration department if you disagree with the findings that were previously sent to you. We wish you luck in finding a suitable organization that can accommodate and advance your career with experimental medications.

Cordially,
Dr. Samuel. P. Longnecker
Medical Director, Bourne Hospital Administration


Lucas Calling sipped his latte while reading the wrinkled termination letter, which was something he did on a daily basis. *Fuck you, Samuel, I'm coming for you*, he thought as he stared at the words. His life had once been full of promise and prosperity, but that changed. The termination letter sent him on a notorious voyage into an evil abyss where only death and vengeance set precedence. Lucas understood the politics of dancing. What he couldn't accept was the sole responsibility of all the failed medical experiments. Samuel Longnecker, his mentor and friend, should have shouldered some portion of the blame. Instead he shunned Lucas as an outcast, destroying him both professionally and socially. Samuel was responsible, and Lucas planned to make him pay. The price wasn't money or justice in a court. It was something more final. Spilled blood was the only acceptable form of payment.

Lucas thought about the fear that took hold of the citizens of Valentine, Nebraska when he carried out his vengeance on a high ranking police official and the family of another officer. "Brian Jeffers, sorry for your loss," he softly whispered. His face lit up as he recalled the violent end of Sarah Jeffers and her daughter Melissa. The two were much easier targets than he had expected. The beauty of it was that they never saw it coming. Lucas had become proficient at the creation of human masterpieces, and it was all leading up to his final creation. *Enjoy your last days, Samuel,* Lucas thought. He laughed aloud.

A mid-twenties, brunette waitress noticed Lucas' smile and took it as an invitation for conversation.

"Hey, Mr. Smiles, want a refill on the latte?" she asked.

Lucas eyed her with suspicion for a moment. Then he handed her a twenty-dollar bill and said, "No thanks, but if you have change for this, I would appreciate it."

The waitress reached into her apron and pulled out several denominations to complete the request. "Of course. How would you like it?"

Lucas purposely smiled. "All ones, if you have it."

She flashed him a naughty grin. "Hmm, just ones huh? That is an odd request." She pointed out the window. "Unless you're heading down the street."

Lucas winked. "Maybe that's exactly where I'm going." He scooped up the bills and hurried out of the coffee shop.

When Lucas felt the waitress was no longer watching, he reached into his jacket pocket and pulled out a flyer for a local gentleman's club. He peered at the dancer on the front and moistened his lips. *Ah, Jade Blue, you are next to join my collection of masterpieces.*

# Chapter 1

# A Killer in the Crowd

Shauna Holden looked down at the dried blood stains on her shirt and pants. She was already twenty minutes late for her shift at the Pleasure Cove, and to make things worse, it started snowing. "Oh just great," she grumbled as she turned on the windshield wipers. *Well, it is Christmas in North Dakota. Grant is going to be so pissed that I'm late again, regardless of the weather.* She turned the blue Ford Escape into a small driveway behind a large building.

The building had once been a movie theater. It was never a popular place. Customers were a rare sight. The owners eventually gave up, closed the theater doors, and put the place up for sale. The new owners transformed the building into the playground for sin known as the Pleasure Cove. Since its inception, the old fashioned citizens of Marcona tried, without success, to close the gentleman's club down.

Shauna parked close to the building. Grant Nesmith, the manager of Pleasure Cove, was positioned at the bottom of the stairs near the back entrance. He ran his hand through his dark-brown, wavy hair and approached Shauna.

"Why are you so late?" he asked.

Shauna pointed to the visual evidence on her clothes and said, "I had a patient who came into the emergency room. It took longer than I expected."

"I told you before to be here on time, and I told you no excuses!" He pulled a Delase cigar out of his front shirt pocket and lit it.

"Grant, I couldn't help it. I do have another job."

"And I remember telling you what my rules were from day fucking one." Grant grabbed Shauna by the arm, opened the door to the back of the club, and walked her to the entrance of the dressing room. He was much stronger than his slight frame made him look. "This is your last chance. Don't think I can't find another tall blonde who wants to dance and show her ass." He loosened the grip he had on her.

"I'm sorry. It won't happen again. I promise," Shauna said.

Grant rubbed his chin and smiled. "Okay, no more shit. You need to decide if you want to keep this job or if you don't. It's that simple, Shauna." He turned and left without saying another word.

Shauna opened the door to the dressing room and sat down in front of the vanity mirror to apply her makeup. She looked at the face staring back at her. The sight was quite revealing. The shy, innocent girl her family and friends knew had completely vanished. Heavy makeup and fake implants replaced her girl-next-door image, leaving almost next to nothing left of her old life. Shauna originally took the job at the club because her nursing career had not been what she expected. She kept her job at the club because her tips amounted to almost twice as much as her earnings at the hospital. She needed to think seriously about what Grant said regarding her wanting the job or not. *Maybe I'll think about it tomorrow, but tonight I need to dance.*

Shauna reached into her tote bag and pulled out a two-piece, white, leather outfit that she knew would make her big money. She quickly got dressed. Then she made her way backstage. She peeked around the wall at the stage and noticed all the seats were full. Excitement filled her from head to toe as the song came to a close. A combination of catcalls and clapping picked up where the music left off. Shauna waved at the dancer coming off stage. The speakers came to life around her. The energetic voice of Grant Nesmith boomed throughout the nightclub.

"Everyone, this girl is bad, she's beautiful, and she is our favorite blonde. Introducing, Pleasure Cove's main attraction, Jade Blue!"

The music started playing and Jade stepped onto the stage. Her white leather outfit outlined her perfectly toned body. She strutted around, stopping for a moment in front of each man to give him his own personal show. One man in the crowd was particularly amazed at the way Jade Blue was moving to the music. He reached into the front pocket of his dress pants and pulled out a silver money clip that contained a stack of bills. A topless waitress noticed the large amount of cash. She approached him from behind and pressed her tanned, bare breasts against his back before she walked around to meet him face to face.

"Hello, I'm sorry," she lied.

"No problem. I need a drink, and since you happen to have bumped into me, I imagine you can help me with that." He smiled.

"Yes, of course I can. What would you like?"

"I have a special request for you. What's your name, Miss?"

"Cassie."

"Okay, Cassie, I would love to have a Long Island Ice Tea with top shelf liquor and two cherries."

"Sure thing, cutie. Anything else I can offer you?" Cassie arched her back to show off her pierced nipples.

"No thank you." He looked away from Cassie and focused his attention on Jade Blue.

Cassie walked away without saying another word. The man pulled a bill from his money clip and walked toward the stage, forcing his way through a few of the other men, all of whom were way too drunk to protest. Once he was at the end of the stage, he waved the bill at Jade Blue. He stared at her intently. He knew she was the same girl he had watched work at the hospital. He also knew she would be performing at the club that night, which was why he was there. He had very special plans for her.

Jade Blue took off her top, exposing the two red pasties that covered her nipples. Then she spotted the man waving the money and directed her attention his way. She removed her skintight shorts, dropped to her hands and knees, and inched her way to the end of the stage where the man waited. She stood up in front of him, removed her pasties, and slid off her thin, red G-string, revealing her natural beauty.

The man removed the stack of money from his money clip,

set aside two bills, and put the rest in his pocket. He combined the two bills with the one he had been waving at Jade Blue and secured them in the money clip. *This will be your last performance*, he thought. He flipped the money clip on the stage. It landed a few feet away from her.

Jade Blue stared at the man. He was taller than most men she knew, and the khaki shirt he was wearing fit his muscular physique in a most appealing way. His short crew cut made her suspect he was in the military. Ironically, just as she thought that, he did a quick salute, turned, and walked back to his table. She redirected her attention to the men sitting around the stage.

When Shauna finished her routine, the crowd gave her the loudest applause she had ever experienced while working at the Pleasure Cove. A huge smile appeared on her face. She was still smiling as she walked around collecting her tips. Her jaw dropped when she reached the money clip the man with the crew cut had thrown on the stage. There was $300 inside of it. She took a closer look at the engraving on the silver clip. Spelled out in black letters were the words, Death's Calling. *That's odd*, she thought, but she quickly blew it off. She walked off the stage and headed for the dressing room. She was unaware that the man responsible for such a large tip would also be responsible for her sudden departure from the living.

# Chapter 2

# Brian Jeffers

Brian Jeffers finally opened the last of the many boxes that the movers had delivered a few days earlier. He inspected the contents to make certain nothing was damaged, and he thought, *This is all I have left of Sarah and Melissa.* After he was satisfied that all the items were in good condition, he carefully picked up the box and walked through the freshly painted hallway toward his home office. He stopped in front of his youngest daughter's room. The homemade poster on her door almost made him laugh for the first time in months. Victoria had a strong passion for the SpongeBob SquarePants cartoon, and the door to her bedroom was evidence of that. She had been such a trooper through all the pain and suffering. Brian was surprised how resilient she was compared to his oldest daughter Alyssa.

Alyssa reverted to a younger version of herself after the murder of her mother and sister. She began wetting her bed and sucking her thumb. It broke Brian's heart. What worried Brian even more than her age reversal was that she had been so quiet over the previous few weeks—too quiet. Brian set the box down on a small hallway table and stared at Alyssa's closed door. There were no posters hanging up. There wasn't any evidence that would indicate it was the room of a thriving eight-year-old. *Not thriving as of late*, Brian thought. He knocked on the door softly as he opened it.

He looked at his oldest daughter, smiled, and gently asked, "Honey, are you hungry?"

"No, daddy."

Alyssa was lying on her pink twin bed, wrapped up in a matching blanket. She was staring at the television, but not really watching it.

"Are you sure? Nothing to eat at all?"

"Not right now, dad, okay?" she responded with a strained voice.

"Okay, I will come back later."

Brian stepped out of her room and quietly shut the door behind him. His eyes began to water. "It's not fucking fair," he whispered. He picked up the box and stepped into his home office. The room was small but still appropriate for what he was using it for. He put the box down and gazed out the window at the picturesque scene of the snowfall from the previous night. *It looks just like a postcard. This is why I moved us here.*

Their new house was miles away from where the sadistic killer Lucas had gone on a rampage, resulting in the death of Melissa and Sarah. He also murdered Brian's supervisor and then had the balls to steal a detective badge. The killer was never caught. Brian took time off after their deaths, and he moved his remaining family to a suburb, but it just wasn't enough. He and the girls needed a new beginning, so he resigned from his position and took a job in a different state, which was the reason for their latest move.

Brian opened the closet and grabbed his dry cleaning. He stripped the plastic off and looked with satisfaction at the navy blue uniform. He ran his fingers over the department patch on the sleeve. The patch was a lighter shade of blue than the uniform and it featured an inlay design of a white-capped mountain surrounded by a running stream. Desoto Valley, Colorado Police was embroidered in red across the top of the patch. Brian hadn't put a uniform on in several years, but the department required it. *So much for leadership.* He quickly got dressed. Then he reached into an open drawer in the closet and grabbed the new gold-plated badge he would wear moving forward. He clipped it into place and put the rest of his duty belt on.

Brian sat down at the desk and opened the top drawer. The fifty-cent piece was staring up at him. He had originally found it underneath a chair in the living room a few weeks after the murders. He had only kept the coin because it was printed the year he was born. He really didn't believe in good luck, but he figured that a little superstition wouldn't hurt anyone. He put the coin in his pocket, just as he had done each morning since he first found it.

Victoria rushed into the office. "Daddy, you look like a real policeman!"

*Ouch, that hurt,* he thought, but he smiled and said, "Ha! Thank you. I think so too." Brian was a tall man, and at one time he had been physically fit. He had gained a few pounds over the previous few years, and it showed.

"Who's going to watch us today?" Victoria cocked her head.

"Well, remember that nice lady you met last week?" Brian asked.

"Miss Stacey?"

"Yeppers. She will be over in a few minutes. I think she also likes SpongeBob," Brian said.

"She does?" Victoria jumped up and down. "I hope she wants to color with me."

"I'm sure she will. Do me a favor. Play with Alyssa today. She hasn't been feeling very good." Brian kissed her on the cheek.

"Sure, daddy!"

"When I get back from work, maybe we will go out for pizza. You have to be good, though." Brian didn't like the girls to eat junk food, but he made an exception once in a while.

"Yeah, daddy, I will be good."

"Okay, it's settled then. Pizza for good girls tonight."

Brian heard the phone ring in the other room. He hurried to answer it before the machine picked up.

"Hello."

"Chief Jeffers, this is Alfred Whitaker. I'm calling in regards to some kids drinking in the back of the high school."

"Mr. Whitaker, I will be in the office in about twenty minutes, and I will make sure to head over there," Brian said, almost with a smile.

"Chief, apparently the same kids have been drinking at the football games as well."

"I will check it out, Mr. Whitaker. Thank you for your call."

"Thank you, Chief."

"No problem, Mr. Whitaker. That's why I'm here," Brian said before hanging up the phone.

Brian realized that was the first time anyone called him Chief at his new job. *I could get used to this*, he thought. It was a new beginning for everyone, and he needed to concentrate on the future.

Brian heard knocking on the front door. Within a few minutes, the girls' new babysitter was ushering him out. He walked down the stairs, feeling the blistering wind on his face, jumped into the white on black police patrol vehicle, and headed down the street. A black Nissan sedan pulled out from a side street and slipped into traffic a few cars behind Brian.

Brian pulled into the secure driveway of the police station. The driver of the sedan parked across the street in an alley. Then he grabbed a manila envelope off the passenger seat and removed a color photo of the person he was paid to follow. The caller had given him specific directions not to harm Police Chief Brian Jeffers. He would abide by those directions, at least for the moment.

# Chapter 3

# Collection Resurrection

Lucas returned to his rental house on the outskirts of Marcona. The sandy, two-story residence had been his home for the previous few months, ever since his quick exit from Dementia. His attempt to kill his long-time nemesis, Samuel Longnecker, turned out to be a grave disappointment. *Soon that situation will be rectified,* he told himself as he opened the door and disarmed the security alarm.

There were only a few pieces of furniture in the house, which was how Lucas wanted it. He lived simple, figuring it would help him stay alive. He looked around at the sparse space and smiled. *Never complicate things.* He unbuttoned his shirt, exposing the heart-shaped necklace he was wearing. The necklace had taken the place of his prized fifty-cent piece, which he believed was lost inside the Jeffers' residence. *That too will be dealt with.*

Lucas walked down the hallway and opened the door to his left. There was a large oak bookcase against the far wall. Its shelves appeared full, but it was only a facade. He pulled out a gold key from his front pocket and inserted it into a hole on the frame of the bookcase. He smiled when he heard the familiar clicking sound of the lock separating. He put his hands behind the bookcase and pulled the heavy wooden structure away from the wall to expose the hidden door. The narrow entryway looked like it had recently been installed, and it was covered in a fresh coat of white paint. He gently turned the silver knob and slowly opened the door. He fumbled for the light switch on the inside of the wall, found it, and flicked it on. The light exposed a spiral staircase. He took hold of the handrail and walked down the stairs. Once he made it to the final step, he reached out to turn on another light switch. *Next time I will bring a flashlight.* The two halogen overhead lights revealed a macabre setting. The walls of the small room were covered with various graphic newspaper clippings that highlighted his masterpieces. He saw his victims as creative works of sadistic art. It pleased him to share his chosen few with the rest of the world.

Lucas walked forward two steps and stopped in front of a large glass cabinet. Inside, there were miniature drawers that looked very similar to the old-fashioned card catalogs found in most modern-day libraries. Each was labeled with a name that corresponded with a newspaper clipping on the wall. Lucas looked at the drawers. *My wonderful collection.* He touched the drawer labeled, Melissa Jeffers, and gently ran his fingers over the heart-shaped necklace he was wearing. The necklace was Melissa's contribution to his collection of death. He was grateful for such a gift.

Lucas stooped over a small table on the other side of the room and picked up a black label maker. He punched several letters into the device, and within a few seconds, another name printed out. The name on the shiny plastic was Shauna Holden. He reached underneath the table and picked up a black duffel bag that contained an assortment of razor-sharp blades and slowly unzipped it, being careful to avoid an accident. It would be quite unfortunate, not to mention painful, if he were injured by his own accessories. He removed all of his tools, one by one, until the bag was empty. Then he sorted out what he needed for that night's special occasion and put those items back in the bag. He left the rest on the table. He walked to the mini-fridge at the edge of the room, opened it, and grabbed two syringes of his paralytic concoction. *Ah, the lovely Propaganician.* Experimental medications had been his specialty and as of late were his trademark signature. He placed the syringes on top of the other items and sealed the bag.

Lucas went back upstairs with his bag in tow and locked up the house before leaving. He was filled with excitement as he left, thinking, *It's almost time to add to the newspaper clippings. Almost time to add a new plastic name tag on a box. Most importantly, it is almost time for the resurrection of my collection.*

# Chapter 4

# Shauna's Final Shift

Shauna walked up to the front entrance of Marcona Memorial Hospital. The sliding doors didn't open. The freezing weather had iced over the automatic entry and sealed it shut.

"Come on, open up bastard," Shauna said as she pounded on the door, trying to get the security officer's attention. "Tim, hey, can you hear me?" She hit the door once more. It still didn't budge.

Tim Spangler, the hefty middle-aged hospital security officer, looked up from the walk-through metal detector and smiled. He braced himself against the glass and forced it open.

"What, is it cold out there?" he jokingly asked.

"Ha, thanks," Shauna said sarcastically as she rubbed her cold, bare hands together. She stepped past Tim and set her pink tote bag on the X-ray scanner conveyor belt.

"You're welcome. Been having trouble with that thing all day, Jade." He winked at Shauna as she took off her brown leather coat.

"What did you just call me?" Shauna raised her eyebrows and gave Tim a playful look.

"I'm sorry. I didn't mean anything by it." He lowered his head to hide his embarrassment.

"Tim, let's keep this between us, okay?" Shauna walked through the medical detector, thinking, *It will suck if any of my supervisors find out.*

"It was me and a few other guys from around town. Nobody from here was with us," Tim assured her. He picked up the tote from the conveyor belt and handed it to Shauna. "I won't tell anyone."

"Good. I figured someone would see me working there, but I didn't think—"

"—What? Because I'm just an old, fat, married guy?"

"No, I just thought you didn't hang out at those places."

"I didn't think you would either," Tim said.

"Ah, point taken." Shauna leaned in close to Tim's ear and whispered, "I owe you a dance." Then she walked away.

Shauna headed down the hallway to the elevator. The elevator door opened right as she reached it. She stepped inside and pushed the button for her floor.

Shauna got off the elevator on the sixth floor and entered the restroom. She was still a little shocked that someone had recognized her at the club. Before her conversation with Tim, she thought she was doing a good job concealing her part-time gig.

Shauna took off her wig, reached into her tote, and pulled out a medium-length, red-haired wig to replace the short-haired one she had been wearing. She slipped it on and adjusted it, ensuring it covered her natural hair. Most people had no idea that she was a blonde. *Now that's $300 well* *spent*, she thought as she looked at herself in the mirror. She grabbed an oversized, green scrub shirt and slid it on over her t-shirt. *Gotta hide the girls.* She chuckled. She adjusted her pants and put on unattractive, dark-rimmed glasses. They were purely cosmetic, but it was a perfect accessory to fit her nerdy nurse profile.

Shauna took the stairs back to the first floor and entered the emergency room. When Nurse Jennifer Mack saw Shauna walk in, she quickly motioned for her.

"Hey, you're just in time. We have a few patients to check in. You get the guy with a broken wrist."

"Lucky me," Shauna said in jest.

"Be happy you didn't get the guy with the irregular bowel," Jennifer said. A mischievous grin appeared on her face.

Shauna grabbed a clipboard and went to the admitting area. The clerk on duty was Felisha Monroe. She was a tall, skinny, know-it-all who didn't like anybody.

*Shauna stepped up to Felisha's desk and asked,* "Do you have the paperwork for the broken wrist?" She tapped on the clipboard.

"I'm busy. You need to wait a minute."

"Felicia, I need it so we can do vitals."

"Gimme a sec. I will find it when I'm ready."

"Okay, I will just tell Doc that you're too busy."

Felicia gave Shauna an I don't give a shit look and handed her two pieces of folded paper. "There you go. I forgot the papers were sitting right in front of me."

"Thanks." Shauna took the paper.

Shauna really disliked Felicia's rude behavior, but she just shrugged it off because whenever anyone filed a complaint about the clerk, it was always pushed under the table.

Shauna went back to the emergency room and tended to several patients for issues ranging from spider bites to chest pains. A few hours later she glanced down at her watch and saw that it was almost 10:00 p.m., which meant it was almost time for lunch. Shauna always thought that lunch so late at night was strange, and it was horrible for her body clock, but late meals were a part of working night shifts. She quickly finished writing her notes regarding her last patient while she waited for the next few minutes to pass. When the clock struck ten, she headed toward the cafeteria.

Before Shauna made it to the cafeteria, she ran into her supervisor, Gloria Stephens. Gloria was a true nurse cliché with her ancient stethoscope, old school nurse dress, and her matching white cap, all of which had gone the way of the dinosaur.

"Shauna, I've been looking for you," Gloria said. "I just got a call from upstairs. One of the ICU patients died a few hours ago. They need a nurse to transport the body to the morgue."

"Don't they have people up there to help? I was on my way—"

"—No, they said they were short on staff. I just need you to drop the body off."

"Is there someone to help me?" Shauna cocked her head to emphasize her question.

"Should be someone down there to help." Gloria walked away. Without looking back, she said in a loud, artificially sweet tone, "Thanks. You're such a dear."

Gloria turned the corner and was well out of sight before Shauna had a chance to say anything else. It was obvious that Shauna had no choice but to go transfer the body as ordered.

Felicia let out an obnoxious laugh. Gloria and Shauna had been talking near the admitting area. Felicia eavesdropped on the entire conversation.

"Bite me, Felicia," Shauna said.

Shauna walked over to the elevator and pushed the button for the ICU. Within a minute, she was standing in front of a large gray desk. The two nurses sitting behind the desk barely recognized the world was in motion as they typed away on their computers.

"Hi, I'm here to pick up . . ." *Shit, I forgot.* Shauna looked down at the paperwork. ". . . Mr. Hundel."

A young, twenty-something, blonde woman looked over her screen and said, "Great. Thank you so much. We are so busy."

"I heard. Where is he?"

"Room 617. He's ready to go."

"Okay, thanks."

Shauna went to room 617. She lightly tapped on the door in case a family member of the deceased happened to be inside saying goodbye. When nobody answered, she opened the door and saw Mr. Hundel's body lying on a stretcher. She pushed the stretcher into the elevator and rode down to the basement, which was where the morgue was located.

The elevator stopped moving, and the doors opened. Shauna looked out at what she knew was the basement hallway, but she was met with complete darkness. "Fucking great! Where are the lights?" she wondered aloud. She pushed the stretcher out of the elevator and placed it against the wall. Having only been down there once before, she wasn't sure where the light panel was located. She walked several feet along the right side of the wall, trying to take advantage of the small amount of light that was radiating out from the inside of the elevator, but she didn't find a switch. The elevator door closed, taking with it the only light. "Shit! I can't believe this." She frantically reached for the up button on the wall, but the elevator was already heading to the floors above her. *Maybe I will just wait here until it comes back*, she thought, but then her panic took over. The hairs on her arms stood straight up. Light beads of sweat formed on her forehead. "I need to get outta here," Shauna shrieked. All of a sudden the ceiling lights started flickering on and off. After a couple of seconds the flickering stopped, and the lights turned on. An amber glow illuminated the hallway. Shauna let out a sigh of relief.

Shauna grabbed the stretcher and pushed it up an incline and through the double doors of the morgue. The odor of bleach and cheap automatic fragrance dispenser greeted her, almost making her nauseous.

"Hello, is anyone here?" Shauna called out. She parked the stretcher in front of the dual storage refrigeration unit. "Hello, anybody here?" she called out again.

Shauna looked around for a staff member. She turned into a short hallway, figuring the attendant might be in one of the side offices. All of the doors were closed. *This is unfucking believable.* She turned her head in each direction as she tried to figure out where to go next. She spotted a phone on the wall a few feet away from her. She walked over to it, picked up the handset, and dialed her supervisor's extension.

"Gloria Stephens."

"Hey, Gloria, it's Shauna. I'm down in the morgue. There's nobody here."

"Shauna, stay put. I just talked to the attendant."

"Huh?"

"Honey, he just called me. Maybe he stepped out. Wait there. He should be back."

"I will wait five minutes, Gloria! That's it! This place is a little creepy."

"You will be fine."

Shauna hung up the phone and rushed back to the main room. She froze in place when she got there. One of the two refrigeration units was wide open, and the body she had brought down wasn't where she had left it. *Run for the door. Just run.* She bolted for the entrance, but she never made it. Lucas anticipated her move and lunged at her from behind the other cooling unit. He grabbed her shoulders and drove her face-first onto the waxed floor. The force of the takedown was so violent that Shauna almost bit completely through her tongue, causing blood to cascade down her scrubs and onto the floor. Instantly, her head snapped back, and as it did, the back of her skull hit Lucas and shattered his nose.

"Dumb bitch," Lucas yelled.

Blood dripped from Lucas' nose, painting the floor with droplets of crimson. He reached into the front pocket of his cargo pants and withdrew the syringe of his creation. Shauna was barely conscious as she tried to crawl closer to the door. She didn't even feel the pointed metal when it penetrated her skin. Lucas pushed the plunger on the syringe, draining the entire contents into her body. Shauna's breathing became shallower. Within several seconds, it was non-existent.

Lucas retreated to the refrigeration unit, grabbed the stretcher, and brought it back to where Shauna was lying. He dumped the corpse onto the floor and placed Shauna's body on the stretcher. He covered her with a blanket, rolled her out of the morgue, and then up a small ramp to the side dock where he had parked his sport utility vehicle, thinking it was the best place for privacy.

Lucas opened the rear SUV door. He yanked Shauna off the stretcher and tossed her in the back of the vehicle. *Nobody will be making rounds for a few hours.* He reached into the glove box, grabbed a small box of Kleenex, and stuffed a few wads up his nose to stop the bleeding. *Tonight's work was sloppy. Very sloppy.* He would take care of the mess later. Collecting from Shauna Holden was his only agenda at the moment. He had the perfect spot in mind for the police to find his new masterpiece.

# Chapter 5

# Killer in Marcona

Kelli Jordan was on the last lap of her run. The Marcona High School running track was open to the public, and she always took advantage of it. The day was so cold that she probably should have run inside on the treadmill, but that wasn't her style. Kelli increased her speed. The former Marine Corps officer and lanky collegiate athlete wouldn't let a little ice and cold weather keep her from her daily ritual. She turned the final corner and finished strong. A quick glimpse of her sport watch had her time recorded at nine minutes and forty-six seconds. *Pretty darn good for a thirty-something-year-old,* she thought.

Kelli slowed to a brisk walk and ripped off her thermal ski mask. She rubbed a gloved hand through her long, black hair. *Okay, now it's cold.* She hustled off the track and headed for the snow-covered parking lot. She opened the door to the gray Lumina and noticed her digital pager in the cup holder was flashing red. *I'm on vacation.* She forcefully grabbed the source of her annoyance and stared at the number on the screen. *End of vacation.* She grabbed her cell from her coat on the passenger seat and dialed the number that was on the pager. A man answered before the second ring.

"Well guess who decided to call us back," the man said.

"I'm on vacation. What's up, Craig?"

"You know where the Pleasure Cove is?"

"Sure, down on Bank Avenue. Give me like fifteen minutes to get there." Kelli shoved the car into gear.

"Kelli, it's a bad one. Somebody sliced up this girl pretty fucking nasty."

"Who is all there?"

"Nobody yet. A patrol unit saw an open door on a vehicle. She was inside. I have a few officers canvassing for witnesses."

"Okay, I'm pulling into my driveway now. Does Chief know you called me?" Kelli asked, knowing she was on the shit list.

"He is aware. He said to use all resources. I gotta go. See you when you get here."

"Gotcha. Be there soon."

Kelli knew that Craig Berte would not have called her unless something was seriously fucked up. The Marcona Police Department had enough capable detectives to handle a murder, so she figured the case he called her about had to be really big. *So much for my vacation. Maybe next time I will spend my vacation somewhere warm.*

Kelli pulled the Lumina into the side street that led to the back parking lot of the Pleasure Cove. A city officer was positioned at the lot's entrance. He was bundled up in a black uniform parka that had a yellow police patch embroidered on the right, front chest pocket. Kelli rolled down the window and held her badge up to the officer for inspection.

"Detective Jordan looking for Detective Berte," she said.

"Go ahead and pull into the lot over there. He's over by the blue Ford Escape," the officer said as he pointed at the area marked off with yellow police tape.

"Thanks."

Kelli parked her car. She spotted Craig next to the sport utility vehicle. He was a rotund man in his mid-forties with short, slightly balding hair.

Craig motioned for Kelli to join him at the vehicle. She quickly walked over.

"Nice car," Kelli said.

"Not on the inside," Craig responded with a sneer on his face.

Kelli took note that all the windows in the Escape were covered with the same charcoal-colored emergency blankets that were found in the back of most patrol units.

"Take a look. Whoever did this is a sick fuck." Craig opened the rear driver's side door.

Kelli peered into the back seat and immediately covered her mouth from the stench of defecation and expelled body fluids. The body of a female was sitting upright in the seat directly behind the driver's seat. Her mouth had been sewn shut, and a ring of bruises surrounded her thin neck. Kelli cocked her head and looked at the woman's chest.

She turned to her partner and asked, "What's missing here?"

"I think our victim used to have implants. I don't think she was that flat before last night," Craig answered.

"Why would anyone take those?"

"I don't know. Maybe some sicko boyfriend or lover wanted his investment back."

"So, this guy slices her, sews her mouth shut, steals her tits, and then decides to leave her in back of the SUV?" Kelli raised both eyebrows.

"I told you it was bad, but you gotta see something else. Come over to my car."

They walked several feet to his blue sedan.

Craig opened the front passenger side door and said, "Pick up the brown bag."

Kelli lifted the small sack and peered inside. "What is this stuff?" Without waiting for an answer, she sorted through the plastic bagged items and saw a red wig, green scrub shirt, and a set of dark-rimmed glasses. "Was this in the car with her?"

"Spot on as usual," Craig answered. He took the bag from Kelli and placed it back on the front seat of his car. "I think our little girl over there was trying to hide her identity from someone."

"You mean the someone who killed her?"

"You're two for two now. I also think we may have a suspect," Craig said in a matter of fact voice.

"Who are we looking at?" Kelli asked as the two returned to the dead girl's car.

"About two nights ago there was a little pissing match between her and the club's manager." Craig reached into his winter coat and pulled out a white notepad. "The guy's name is Grant Nesmith."

"Sounds like you have this case figured out. How about letting me go back on vacation?" Kelli coaxed.

"I need you on this one."

"How many people verified the argument between those two?" Kelli asked.

"Just two that we know of. She still performed after they got into it."

Kelli looked at the body once more and felt pity for the girl. She hoped Craig was right about the murder being spawned out of rage, but somehow Kelli thought someone more sinister was responsible for such mutilation, and it truly worried her.

**Chapter 6**

# Unseen Enemy

Police Chief Brian Jeffers had been searching the police database for an hour. All of the juveniles taken into custody by the patrol units that day had lengthy records. Brian stood at his doorway and waved for the last remaining offender.

"Scott, come in here," Brian said sternly.

Scott popped out of the chair and strutted into Brian's office.

Scott Jepsen was seventeen years old. He dropped out of high school during his first semester because he wanted to play Xbox instead of doing anything educational. He was prison camp skinny. His oversized red sweater and baggy blue jeans didn't really do anything for him. Brian guessed the acne on his face hadn't been taken care of for years.

"You can't take me to jail; I'm too young." Scott shoved both hands in his pockets.

Brian shut the door behind him and straightened his uniform tie. Then he asked, "How sure of that are you?"

"I know what you cops can do. I'm a minor, so just call my dad."

"Scott, the thing is, drinking in public is sort of a big deal since you're underage." Brian tapped his desk with a pencil.

"Give me a ticket then. You can't keep me here."

"Well, actually, I can. I had Officer White contact your father at work. Guess what he thinks should happen?"

"Nothing. My dad has money, and you know how it goes." Scott puffed his chest out at Brian.

"Unfortunately, I do, but this time the police department is going to process you for the offense. I already called juvenile services."

"Not cool man. Can't you just throw down a ticket on me?" Scott pleaded.

"I don't think so, Scott. Unlike you, Jacob and Michael were cooperative and took responsibility for their actions." Brian baited the youngster.

"Are they going to juvie too?" Scott began chewing on his nails.

"No. Those two admitted to me that you got the beer for them. Officer White is waiting for their parents to come get them." Brian leaned back in his chair and waited for the boy to cave in.

"Okay, can you get me out of the juvie thing? I hear bad things happen there." Scott's tough exterior was beginning to melt.

"Here is what I will do, Scott. I will let you off with a citation for possession of alcohol, and I won't charge you for public intoxication. There is one condition—"

"—Okay, what is it?"

"If you are caught again doing anything illegal, and I mean

it when I say anything, you will be sent to juvenile services, without hesitation." Brian handed the boy a citation that had already been filled out. "Understand?"

"Yes, I understand." Scott answered.

Brian opened the door, and Scott quickly got up and walked out.

"Have a good day," Brian said. Then he slammed the door shut before Scott could utter a protest. *Maybe that kid won't be in here again*, he hoped.

Brian retreated to his desk. He took a quick glance out the window as he sat down. *That's two days in a row now.* He picked up his desk phone and dialed Officer Cordell White's extension number.

"Officer White."

"Cordell, are you busy?"

"No. Those two are cooling their jets in the lobby. What's up, boss?"

"Come in my office. I want to show you something," Brian said as he peeked out the window.

"I will be there in a minute, boss."

Brian heard a harsh knock on his door. He looked up and saw Cordell as he had expected. Officer Cordell White was a fifty-year-old, part-time farmer and a twenty-year veteran of the police department. He had a dark complexion and brownish-gray hair.

"Hey, Brian, what's going on? What did you want to show me?" Cordell asked.

"Check out the sedan on the side street over there. I didn't think anything of it yesterday, but it's here again."

"You want me to send a unit to drive by?" Cordell asked.

"Maybe I'm just being paranoid, but it's a little strange." Brian squinted as he tried to read the license plate. It was too far away for him to make out the numbers.

"All cops are paranoid. Shit, I'm the king of paranoia, so don't feel bad." Cordell reached into his right uniform pants pocket and pulled out a set of mini-binoculars. "Let's see who this guy is."

Brian pointed at the binoculars and jokingly said, "So if we get a complaint of a voyeur in the neighborhood, we know it's you."

"Ha, very funny."

Cordell focused his binoculars on the sedan's license plate. "Brian, here is the plate. It's a Nebraska personalized plate with the letters I, L, I, V, E."

"Let's run it through the database," Brian said.

Brian typed the vehicle information into the system. Thirty seconds later, he knew who owned the vehicle. He tapped the print screen button, and the laser jet spat out the printed sheet.

"Cordell, get a patrol unit out there!" Brian ordered.

Brian jumped up and pulled out his nickel-plated 9mm semi-automatic Mazre duty weapon. Then he flung open the door and ran out the rear exit of the office. Cordell rushed out the door to follow him.

"Brian, where are you going?" Cordell shouted. He hit the transmit button on his portable radio. "Units 706 and 709, meet the chief and me in the alley off Harris and Thirteenth."

Brian reached the alley and positioned himself behind a

parked car. *Not the ideal spot, but it will do.*

Cordell caught up to him. He was visibly out of breath.

Brian pushed the talk button on his radio and said, "Units 706 and 709, come in from the opposite side of the alley. White and I have him boxed off. Be advised, the subject has outstanding warrants for five homicides."

"Brian, who is this guy?" Cordell asked. He was finally regaining his wind.

"Ronald Trapp. A few years ago he kidnapped a girl in the city where I used to work."

Brian raised his weapon and aimed it at the driver's side window. The dark tint obscured his view, making it impossible to see if anyone was inside.

The two patrol units arrived and blocked off the man's only escape route.

Cordell sensed something more was bothering Brian. He picked up his radio and called the patrol units again. "Units 706 and 709, we are moving to the vehicle. Give us a little cover fire," Cordell said with panic in his voice.

Brian reached out and grabbed Cordell by the wrist. "Cordell, all I know is this man has killed a lot of people. We need to bring him down."

Brian moved away from the parked car and advanced toward the vehicle. Cordell followed behind him.

"Here we go, 706 and 709," Cordell yelled.

Brian rushed for the sedan with his weapon ready. *Why would this man be here if he wasn't trying to kill the rest of my family? This has to be the guy.* He dove for the ground as a ring of gunfire cut through the bitter cold. The barrage of metal seemed to last forever, but in reality, it was just seconds. Brian Jeffers didn't feel the two rounds that penetrated his uniform or the path each made when they struck his tactical vest. He drifted into darkness where a peaceful sleep awaited him.

# Chapter 7

# A Visit from Samuel

Lucas removed two white plastic bags from his duffel bag. He gently opened the first and pulled out the liquid filled pouch that had been Shauna's breast implant. He wiped off the remaining blood with a green hand towel. Then he opened a drawer and carefully placed the breast implant in the back of it so that there was room for the other one. He picked up the other white bag and repeated the procedure. When he was finished, he shut the drawer and put the label in place. *Shauna Holden is now a part of my collection.* He closed the glass case and turned off the lights to his workshop.

Lucas returned to the upper level of the house with his tools in hand and stepped in front of the kitchen sink. He grabbed a small bottle of washing powder and started scrubbing. It only took him a few minutes to complete the task. He left the tools to dry on a few paper towels. Then he walked over to the full-length mirror outside his bedroom. He smiled as he looked at himself. The green scrubs he was wearing had a few crimson stains, but he could get those out by using the right mixture of bleach and soap. *I might want to use these again*, he thought. He reached into the single rear pocket and removed the plastic card that had gained him access to the hospital's rear dock. *Too easy. Just too easy.* He stripped off his clothing and walked into the bathroom to check his nose. He extracted the tissue from each nostril and was relieved to see that the blood had finally clotted. Darkness was forming underneath his eyes. *There will definitely be bruises by morning, but it will heal.* He grabbed his black robe off the rack and shoved the soiled clothing into the hamper.

Lucas picked up a copy of The Eagle, which was the city of Marcona's newspaper, and thumbed through it until he located a specific article. The article featured the esteemed Dr. Samuel Longnecker and his newfound success with the usage of experimental medications. It also detailed his agenda for the trip he would soon be making to Marcona. The doctor was scheduled to do an interview with the local Marcona radio station and attend a benefit dinner at the Darien Auditorium. *Such a fucking liar. Only a few days left and you're mine.* Lucas sneered, wadded up the paper, and threw it against the wall. *I will not fail this time.* The ringing of his prepaid cell phone interrupted his thoughts. He reached into his jacket. Only one person had that phone number.

"Ronald, what is it?"

"Patrick, something bad went down here," Ronald Trapp said.

Patrick was the alias Lucas went by when dealing with Ronald.

"What?" Lucas took a deep breath. "Ronald, tell me what happened."

"The detective guy you told me to keep an eye on . . . he made me . . . I had to do—"

"—What did you do, Ronald?" Lucas asked, raising his voice.

"Patrick, I think he's dead," Ronald said. His voice sounded shaky.

"You were just told to watch him."

"He rushed the car. I fired my gun. I think I killed them all."

"What car are you talking about, Ronald?" Lucas clenched his teeth. *Fucking idiot. Probably his own car.*

"My car . . . I didn't think he would find out," Ronald said sheepishly.

"You didn't think a former homicide detective would figure out a wanted piece of shit like you was following him?" Lucas was breathing hard. *I knew this guy couldn't do an easy fucking job.*

"I don't know what to say, Patrick." Ronald's voice drifted off.

"Did you at least get the item I told you about?"

"No. I bolted in the car. I'm sure nobody else saw me."

*Fat chance*, Lucas thought. "Okay, so you completely fucked up everything you could."

"No. I did what you told me," Ronald whined.

"I need you to come to Marcona. We need to figure out what we're going to do."

Lucas already knew. It was going to be quite unfortunate—at least for Ronald.

"Maybe I can still get the item you want," Ronald pleaded.

"Don't worry about that now. Just head back here."

"I will be there late tonight," Ronald said.

"That will be fine. See you then." Lucas disconnected the call.

*Ronald's screw-up is unforgivable. At least he doesn't know my real name. Ronald will pay, and then Samuel will pay.* Lucas smiled. He always enjoyed thinking about adding to his collection.

# Chapter 8

# The Nesmith Interview

A silver Mercedes slid in behind the black and gold Marcona Police marked unit. Detective Kelli Jordan took a final drag from her cigarette and tossed it out the window. *Stupid habit. Maybe I'll quit someday.* Craig had been called away for another case at Marcona General Hospital, so he left Kelli with the task of interviewing Grant Nesmith. *Not a good way to start the day,* Kelli thought as she stepped out of the car.

Kelli walked up to the man standing by the Mercedes and said, "Hello, Mr. Nesmith."

"Where's Shauna?" he asked.

"Sir, do you have an office where we can talk privately?"

"Yes. It's on the second floor."

Grant led Kelli through the back entrance and up a flight of stairs. He removed a red plastic card from inside his shirt pocket and waved it in front of a matching card reader. *A lot of security for a strip club,* Kelli thought. She pulled out her notebook and jotted down a few words. Grant Nesmith noticed her taking notes so he offered an explanation.

"We have more than average sales here, and we just put

in a wall safe. There's a lot of cash in this place, so security is important."

"I see," Kelli said. She was still suspicious of the man.

The door opened. Kelli followed Grant to his office. The man's office was impressive. The large room had wall to wall black fur carpet, a full service built-in bar, a cherry wood desk topped with a desktop computer and widescreen monitor, a luxurious looking leather desk chair, and an extra wide cherry wood conference table with matching chairs. The numerous gold-framed wall prints scattered on the maroon walls were what stood out the most. The artwork was quite intricate and appeared to be replicas of the female dancers employed by the club.

"Detective, the other officer wanted to speak with me about Shauna. Is she all right?" Grant asked.

"No. Tragically, Ms. Holden was found dead in her car outside in this parking lot." Kelli flipped to a blank page in her notebook.

Grant was clearly caught off-guard. He looked genuinely surprised and shaken up.

"When?" he asked with a weak voice.

"Today. We understand the two of you had a little spat in front of the dressing room." Kelli perched herself against the conference table.

"It was nothing major."

"Some people thought it was significant enough to tell us," Kelli said.

"Like I said, it was nothing."

"Mr. Nesmith, if it was nothing, then you shouldn't have a

problem telling me about it." Kelli clicked her ballpoint pen.

"People here think I had something to do with her death?"

"You're putting words in my mouth. They saw you have an altercation with the deceased." Kelli jotted down a few notes. "Just give me an idea of what happened."

Grant shifted in his seat. "I told her not to be late again. She was late three out of the last seven days she worked."

"She was upset because of that?" Kelli penned out a few more sentences.

"No. I told her any blonde could walk in here and shake her ass for money. That probably upset her."

"You think?" Kelli scribbled in her book. "So, a few people see you guys in this argument, and now the girl is dead." Kelli noticed Shauna Holden's picture on the wall.

"Like I said, it wasn't that big of a deal. She went out on stage and performed. I thought everything was cool."

"Was she involved with drugs, alcohol, maybe both?" Kelli asked, but she didn't think the girl looked like the typical drug user.

"Shauna had another job . . . a nursing job, but we didn't know where."

"Don't the employees have to give that info out?"

"We don't generally care about other jobs, but in her case it was becoming a problem." Grant opened his bottom desk drawer, pulled out a blue folder, and held it out for Kelli as he said, "Here is Shauna's personnel folder. I'm sure you'll need it. It has an address. Maybe this will help you."

*A personnel folder for someone working in an X-rated tittie bar? You gotta be kidding,* Kelli thought as she took the folder.

She opened it and flipped through the pages. There was a city address listed on the contacts page. She scrawled it down and inspected the remaining papers.

"Mr. Nesmith, do you know if she had family, friends, maybe a boyfriend she talked about?"

"Never mentioned anyone to me. Wasn't what I would call a very congenial girl. We hired her because she was the best performer, and the men left here happy."

*I bet they did*, Kelli thought. "So nobody here ever talked to her at all?" she asked in disbelief.

"Not really. Shauna was the headliner here. Most of the other girls would love to be in her position."

"Love it enough to kill for the spot?" Kelli didn't wait for a response. She closed the notebook, stood up, and pointed to the framed prints. "I need to interview all the women who still work here."

Grant gritted his teeth. "I understand."

"That also includes a statement from you. I also need to pull the security tapes for review."

"I'm not going to let you have those without a court order. Our customers are some of the most elite businessmen and influential people—"

"—I'll get an order. Spare me the political ramification bullshit." Kelli opened the door.

Grant stood up to escort Kelli out. He looked at her and said, "Detective, I hope you can understand my position."

"What I understand is simple. A girl is dead, and her body was sitting in the parking lot where she worked." Kelli's cell phone vibrated. She detached the phone from her belt and answered the call. "Detective Jordan," she said.

"Kelli, its Craig. I need you to come to Marcona General. The dead girl worked here, and I found something."

"What?" Kelli asked.

"I'll show you when you get here."

"Okay, I'm leaving now. This guy wants us to subpoena the security tapes."

"Not surprised. Hustle over here, okay?"

Kelli ran to her car, jumped inside, and turned on the emergency lights so she could drive full speed. *Craig sounded like he might have some answers. Hopefully they are the right ones*, she thought.

# Chapter 9

# Not Dead

Brian Jeffers couldn't understand why he still had conscious thoughts surging through his head, and it wasn't the whole life flashing before your eyes before being thrust back into the land of living concept that others talked about. He was processing the last few minutes up to the shooting. *This is what death is like? This might be hell . . . reliving the moments of death constantly, day after day, for eternity.*

Pain suddenly radiated throughout Brian's chest and he heard a soft, steady hum. The hum became increasingly clearer. Then Brian heard voices surrounding him. He listened intently.

"I think he's coming around," someone said.

"I'll get the doc," a softer voice said.

"Brian, can you hear me? It's Rich. You're gonna make it."

Rich, better known as Delano Valley's Mayor Richard Storm, was notified of the shooting right after it happened. He listened to the police scanner to find out more information. When he heard there was a survivor, he drove straight to the hospital.

"Brian," Rich repeated, "You're going to be okay."

Brian recognized Rich's voice and realized he was still alive. The pain was forcing him out of his unconscious state. His eyes began to flutter. Then his eyes opened. The harsh fluorescent lighting replaced the darkness. Brian squinted while his pupils adjusted. He slowly moved his head down and glimpsed at the assortment of colored wires attached to his chest. He followed the wires to a small monitor, which was the source of the humming he had heard. *I'm not dead. I'm in the hospital.* He looked up and smiled at the white-haired, short man leaning against his bed.

"I need more drugs," Brian whispered.

Richard Storm's worried look turned into one of relief. "The doctor should be here in a minute. We will get you taken care of."

"How are my girls doing? Did anybody tell them what happened?" Brian asked.

"They're with your new sitter. She told them you were injured at work. That's all. Nothing about the shooting."

"Is the bastard dead?"

"Brian, bad news." A few tears slid down both sides of Richard's face. "You're the only one left. Cordell, Andrew, and Mike are gone." He put his hand on Brian's shoulder.

"I'm sorry. This guy was ready for us." Brian choked back a few tears.

"The man got away before more units could be dispatched. There is an all-points bulletin out nationwide for him," Richard said.

"He was watching me. I think this guy killed my wife and

daughter." Brian's pain was getting worse and the monitor started making loud, high-pitched noises.

"Try to calm down." Richard worriedly watched the monitor.

"I know he was here watching me. I just don't know why," Brian said.

The door opened, and a tall, potbellied, bearded man wearing a white coat approached the bedside. "Mr. Jeffers, I'm Doctor Rose. I see you are awake. I'll order something for the pain. You're a lucky man, by the way."

*Yeah right.* "I don't feel so lucky." Brian clutched at his chest.

"Well, you are. The bullets hit your vest, and the vest slowed down the bullets before they entered your body, and that is why the bullets only damaged your left pectoral muscle. I say you're pretty lucky."

"Guess no push-ups for me," Brian joked.

"No, not for a few months. I hope to get you out within a few days, but we will see." Dr. Rose picked up the chart. "I will check in on you later. The nurse will be coming by with pain meds." Dr. Rose took a glimpse at Brian's wound and left.

"Rich, I don't have anybody to take care of the girls. Would you and your wife mind keeping an eye on them?"

"You don't even have to ask. Get some rest, and listen to the medical staff. I will worry about the press on this. Brian, this guy was well armed. At least 100 rounds fired at you guys.

"Rich, I want to know why he would risk coming to this town. It doesn't make any sense. It just doesn't."

"I don't know either. If this guy was watching you, I don't know what to think." Richard rubbed his chin.

"Unfinished business," Brian said.

"Don't worry about it until you're out of here, okay?"

Brian weakly nodded his head in agreement.

"Get some rest. I will tell the kids you are fine." Richard assured him. "I have to get going. I will come see you later." He walked to the door and turned to wave before he stepped out and closed the door behind him.

Brian knew there would be a heavy dose of backlash and second guessing from the citizens of the community, not to mention the news media. He had thought moving would put the past far behind, but it only followed him. He knew there were answers to why his wife and daughter were murdered and why he was shot. Brian wouldn't stop until he found out what those answers were.

# Chapter 10

# Unforgiving

Lucas turned onto the dark, unpaved alley. He flipped on the high beams to compensate for the lack of lighting and parked the sport utility vehicle behind a debilitated structure that had formerly been Black's Window Emporium.

There was a time when Black's was the biggest producer of high-quality glass and custom-made windows in the area, but the economic downturn, competition from big store brands, and consumer desire for cheap mass produced products brought sales to a halt, so the store closed. The building sat empty for years. Eventually, homeless people took refuge inside the abandoned structure and turned it into a makeshift shelter.

Lucas looked at the trash littered street and thought, *The homeless will mind their own business.* He knew most of them had bad experiences that caused them to distrust society, which meant it was unlikely they would report a crime. *Most people prefer to shoo away the homeless rather than help them.* He turned off the engine and stepped out of the vehicle. Then he walked around to the rear cargo area and opened the door. The interior was covered with a plastic sheet. Lucas ran his hand along the smooth plastic and smiled. Then he grabbed his duffel bag, opened it, and removed a syringe of Propaganician, one of his cutting instruments, and a small tin can containing an oily substance. He opened the tin can and emptied the entire contents onto the plastic sheet. He took one last look at his handiwork. *Everything is in place.* He shut the cargo door with extreme care and stared at the rear of the vehicle for a moment. *It shouldn't leak out. Almost done with the prep work.* Excitement was building up inside of him. He retreated to the front of the SUV, opened the passenger side door, and pulled a screwdriver out of the glove compartment, which he used to remove the license plates. *Now the fun really begins.* He placed the rectangular plates onto the hood of his truck, flipped open his cell phone, and dialed Ronald's number.

"Hello," Ronald answered.

"Hey, Ronald, how far out are you?" Lucas asked.

"I should be there in a few. Why couldn't we just meet in a bar or something?"

"Because we can't. Do you understand? They know what vehicle you have. I'm surprised you have made it this far."

"How are we gonna solve that?" Ronald asked.

*With extreme pain,* Lucas thought. He clenched his teeth as he forced himself to use a pleasant tone of voice. "When you get here, I will take care of it."

"Patrick, I really didn't want to ice those guys. They didn't give me a choice," Ronald admitted.

"I know, but you still pulled the trigger. We have to find a safe place for you right now." *I have one in mind.*

"I'm glad you got my back on this."

"I have another job lined up for you. It's on the other side of the country," Lucas said to distract him.

"Great. I think it will be too hot to do anything here for quite a while."

*Too hot is a good assumption.* Lucas held back his laughter. "No problem. I see your headlights coming up the alley. I'm behind the building to your right."

The sedan stopped in front of Lucas' sport utility vehicle. Ronald climbed out. The sudden exposure to the freezing cold air took his breath away for a second. He inhaled deeply and slowly exhaled. "Fuck, it's cold out here!"

"Yeah, it is. Did you ditch the gun after the shooting?"

"That shit is gone, man. All I have is my semi-auto in the trunk."

"Good. Here is the plan. Give me your cell phone." Lucas reached out.

"Why?" Ronald asked.

*This guy killed eight people? I can't imagine how.* "Because, Ronny, if you are ever caught, you are a link to me, and I can't have that." Lucas stepped closer to him. "I need the phone."

Ronald handed him the phone. "Man, I'm sorry. Had a few lines of coke before I drove here. Guess I'm not thinking."

*Figures.* Lucas took the phone and slipped it inside his coat. "I will do the thinking for both of us." Lucas motioned toward the sport utility vehicle. "Here's what we're going to do. You will take my truck, and I will take your car. I already removed the plates from it. We just need to transfer yours." Lucas hoped that Ronald was too coked-up to realize how illogical his proposal was.

"Gotcha. So you're gonna keep my car, and I get to keep yours?"

"Precisely. Nobody should find you in this vehicle. There's a map inside the glove compartment that shows where I want you to go."

"We just put my plates on the car, and then, that's it?" Ronald asked.

"That's it, Ronny." Lucas handed him the screwdriver. "We need to hurry."

Ronald removed the plates from his sedan and handed them to Lucas.

"Man, it doesn't seem fair that you get my piece of shit car, and I get this nice ride." Ronald ran his hand along the SUV's sleek exterior.

*Not mine anyway.* "Don't worry about it. Just don't get caught."

Lucas finished putting the license plates on the SUV.

"Come help me with the cargo door, Lucas said."

Lucas reached in his coat and slid out the syringe. He cupped his hand around the plastic as Ronald peeked around the corner. *Time to die, Ronald.*

"Big, strong Patrick can't open the door. Now that's funny," Ronald joked.

*I will show you something amusing.* "Very funny. I think it's stuck. Give me a hand," Lucas said.

Ronald grabbed the handle. "Hey, Patrick, do you smell something?" He sniffed the air.

"Yes, I do." Lucas flipped his right hand over and grabbed the syringe containing the paralytic with his left hand.

Ronald saw what was happening but was too slow to stop the needle from entering his throat.

"Ah," Ronald screamed. The harsh wind muffled his cry.

"Easy, Ronald. I told you everything would be taken care of."

Lucas hugged Ronald closer to him and slammed his fist against the syringe, forcing the contents into his flesh. He let go of Ronald and watched intently.

Ronald's eyes widened and then his body collapsed onto the frozen ground. He convulsed several times. Then his body was completely still.

Lucas opened the cargo door and lifted the former killer into the back of the SUV. He gently removed the exhausted syringe from Ronald's throat and tucked it back inside his coat. The stench of lighter fluid filled the vehicle. *Time is of the essence. I need to work quickly*, he reminded himself. He grabbed his knife. With a few strokes of sharpened steel, Lucas shredded Ronald's clothes. He pushed a button on the wall panel to open the storage shelf, reached inside, and pulled out a jar that was partially filled with an opaque liquid. Lucas used his blade on Ronald to cut off two souvenirs for his collection, which he then slid inside the jar. "If you only would have listened to me," Lucas said to Ronald's motionless body.

When Lucas' work was complete, he packed his tools in the duffel bag and slung the bag handles over his shoulder. He pulled a book of matches out of his front pants pocket and took a step away from the SUV. Lucas smiled as he ignited one of the matches and threw it inside the vehicle. The plastic sheet instantly combusted into flames, making short work of Ronald Trapp. Lucas forced the cargo door shut and retreated to his late employee's sedan. *Such a waste of a nice vehicle.*

The inferno of flames dancing against the winter night sky mesmerized Lucas, but not for long. Within a few short moments, the truck exploded, leaving only molten steel and the smell of burned flesh. A sinister grin appeared on Lucas' face. He turned toward Ronald's sedan. *Time to get rid of this vehicle as well.* He had the perfect place to dispose of it, and that's where he was headed.

Lucas looked down at the duffel bag and smiled. Ronald Trapp would no longer be a problem for him. It was time to prepare for Samuel's arrival. *Just about a week away now, Samuel. Only a week until you are one of my masterpieces.*

# Chapter 11

# All in the Blood

Kelli Jordan entered the rear door adjacent to the hospital loading dock. She had to weave through an endless amount of yellow crime scene tape to reach Craig Berte. He was in the middle of a conversation with two men dressed in tan work uniforms. *Must be cleaning employees of some kind,* she thought.

Craig noticed Kelli and waved at her. Then he excused himself from the men and walked up to her.

"Kelli, our victim worked here as an emergency room nurse. Come check this out."

Craig led Kelli through the double doors of the morgue.

Kelli saw the thick patches of blood on the floor. "Shit," she blurted out, "this is the original crime scene?" She bent down to get a closer look.

"I think so. It seems like the guy was waiting for her."

"What, an employee?" Kelli cocked her head.

"I don't think so. I think someone was keeping an eye on her from her other job at the strip club," Craig said in a matter of fact tone.

Kelli stood up and looked at Craig. "You think a stalker

was after her?"

"No. Take a look at this." Craig reached into his jacket and removed a transparent evidence bag. It's a money clip. The cleaning staff found it in the corner of the room." He tossed the bag to Kelli.

"There's writing engraved on it," Kelli said. She squinted to read the letters. "Does that say Death's Calling?"

"Sure does. Maybe the killer was a really jealous, angry ex boyfriend of hers."

Craig pointed in the direction of the wide-open cooling unit and started walking toward it. Kelli followed.

"The manager at the club didn't think she had a boyfriend or significant other," Kelli said.

"He could be wrong. A girl who carries a red wig, over-sized work clothes, and unattractive glasses is hiding from something." Craig escorted Kelli into the cooler.

"I'll give you that, but maybe she was hiding from the people at the hospital." Kelli spotted a naked body on the floor and abruptly stepped back. "Who the fuck is that?"

"He is another weird piece of this murder. According to the toe-tag, his name is Mr. Delvin Hundel. He passed away a few days ago, but someone just left him here on the ground. Apparently the cart the hospital staff uses to haul bodies isn't here." Craig scanned the area.

"Why would they dump him a few feet from . . . " Kelli stopped mid-sentence. She was distracted by the bloated body.

Craig shook his head. "Nobody who worked here would. I spoke with the three employees who work in this area. Every deceased patient is brought down on a cart."

"So the killer wheels her out, up the hallway, and out through the back dock door?" Kelli shook her head. "What the fuck?"

"Exactly what I was thinking, but considering the evidence, it makes sense. Not to mention, this place is pretty sealed. The front entrance has a security post with an X-ray machine and walk-through metal detection unit."

They exited the cooler.

Kelli peered at a blood spatter on the wall and said, "This is a little strange."

"What?" Craig leaned in."

Kelli outlined the trail of blood. "We have a different blood pattern here. Most of the blood is in this area here." She pointed to the floor. "This one is separate from it. Let's get a sample."

"I'll get Andrew from forensics to process it. I have a problem with something else," Craig said as he ushered Kelli out the door and led her to the delivery dock. "Kelli, how did he get access?" He waved his hand in front of a metallic device along the wall. "Look, a card reader. The killer would need valid identification to gain access."

"Maybe a stolen card." Kelli glared at the electronic access device.

"I asked the security director about that. Nothing has been reported lost or stolen for months," Craig said.

"Maybe someone held the door open for him." Kelli shrugged.

"They wouldn't do that unless . . ."Craig's eyes lit up.

"Unless whoever saw him thought he worked here," Kelli said. She inspected the door's magnetic lock. "We need to check for stolen uniforms of any kind."

"If this is like most places, the inventory probably fluctuates," Craig said.

"Probably, but there has to be something we can find."

"I'll have an officer talk to the laundry people. Craig searched the dock for employees.

"It's worth a shot." *This guy planned out the murder well,* Kelli thought.

Craig opened his notebook. "I need you to speak with a Gloria Stephens. She was Shauna Holden's supervisor."

"Sure. Is she around?"

"I checked with her boss and asked if she would come in. She's supposed to be here within the hour," Craig said while he looked at the overhang.

Kelli realized what Craig was looking for. "There's no video camera up there," Kelli said.

"Nothing is ever easy, is it?" Craig asked. He grabbed a digital camera out of his coat pocket and snapped a few pictures. "The security director is pulling the tapes from other areas. Maybe we will get a hit on something."

Kelli smiled. "At least this guy is cooperative." She was still pissed about Grant Nesmith's unwillingness to help.

Craig knew Kelli pretty well and could sense what was bothering her. "Nesmith's an asshole for making us get the court order. Nobody does the right thing anymore, unless they have too."

A young man in a dark suit approached Craig and Kelli.

He looked like a federal agent, but he was actually a medical examiner.

"Detectives, I need to speak with you both, alone," Medical Examiner Kurt Delong said.

The three found a break room in a side office.

*This is odd*, Kelli thought. She knew the medical examiner didn't make a habit of speaking with investigators. A quick blurb on a report was the general protocol.

"Kurt, what did you find?" Craig asked.

"It's quite eerie. There are two issues that concern me. One, under each breast of the victim there are incisions cut at the same depth and length. Essentially, they are perfect."

"Perfect? What do you mean?" Kelli asked.

"I mean the incisions are without flaw. They were created with great surgical skill." Kurt grabbed a brown folder and showed them two photos. "See how the cut is for both?"

"Is that even possible?" Craig asked.

"It rarely happens. It would take a very steady hand to do this, especially in the back seat of a car. The second thing I wanted to show you is in the back of the folder. Check out the blue sheet. That's the lab results."

"What am I looking at?" Craig asked.

"The results showed some abnormalities in her blood," Kurt said.

Kelli glimpsed at the paper. "If I'm reading this right, she had some drugs on board when she died."

Kurt Delong nodded. "One drug, and it's not something you would expect to find. It's a paralytic compound called Propaganician."

Craig stared at the medical examiner.

"Okay, I'm not great with medical terminology, and I'm not even going to try to pronounce whatever you just said, but a paralytic stops movement, right?" Craig asked.

"That's exactly what it does. It's used to pause the breathing process until an artificial device, such as a vent unit, takes over for an intended patient. What's even more interesting is that this particular drug isn't available for public consumption."

"So you wouldn't prescribe this to anyone?" Kelli asked.

"No, not unless they were hospitalized."

"How did it get in her system?" Craig asked.

"It was injected into her. She had a small wound in the back of her neck," Kurt answered.

"Well, if the paralytic caused her to stop breathing, why mutilate the girl?" Kelli shook her head.

"That's something I can't answer." Kurt closed the folder. "I do know a physician or former plastic surgeon made those cuts on her."

"Can someone get the drug easily? Kelli asked.

"No, it is ordered and kept track of. If I find out anything further, I will give you both a call."

Kurt, in a hurry to leave, quickly stowed the paperwork in his briefcase, stood up, and walked out.

"Sometimes that guy gives me the creeps." Craig chuckled.

"But if he's right about what's going on—"

Craig cut Kelli off. "—If he's right, how do you catch a guy like this?"

Kelli held up the plastic bag that contained the money clip. "Maybe this is just what we are looking for."

# Chapter 12

# Devising His Own Demise

 Samuel Longnecker looked out at the snow covered tress and ice-covered ground as he drove. *One more speaking engagement left until I'm home*, he told himself.

The event planner had been most gracious. He gave Samuel first class plane tickets, his choice of a rental vehicle, and the most impressive lodging he had ever seen.

Samuel turned into the circular driveway in front of Jos Glades. He stared in awe. *This is even more stunning in real life.*

The sixty-story, Victorian style hotel had all the modern necessities one could possibly ask for, yet it still managed to keep a 19th century flair.

Samuel stopped the car under the canopy, almost in shock at how quick the valets were. A young, thin man wearing a white and gold, trimmed uniform, appeared to be eagerly awaiting his arrival.

*The valet walked up to Samuel's window and said,* "Good morning, Sir. Welcome to Jos Glades."

"Thank you, I'm Samuel Long—"

"—Mr. Longnecker," the valet interrupted, "we have been expecting you. Marisa is inside waiting to assist you." He opened the driver's side door for Samuel. "You can leave your keys, Sir. I will take care of your automobile."

"Well, thank you," Samuel said, impressed with how spot-on the young man was.

Another valet appeared and said, "Welcome, Sir. May I carry your luggage?"

"No thank you." Samuel grabbed his suitcase out of the car. "I only brought one piece of luggage. I can manage just fine. I do, however, appreciate the offer." Samuel turned to the first valet. "My keys are in ignition, and again, thank you."

Samuel headed for the check-in desk with his suitcase in tow. An exotic Middle Eastern woman intercepted him.

"Mr. Longnecker, what an honor to have you here. My name is Marisa, and I will be here to assist you with anything you need." She handed him a gold envelope. "Your key card and itinerary, Sir."

"Thank you!"

"You're certainly welcome. Mr. Longnecker. Would you like an escort to your suite?" she asked as she walked him to the glass elevator.

"No, that won't be necessary. I can manage on my own. I would like to say that you do have an exquisite hotel here." The elevator doors opened and he stepped inside. He turned around to face, Marissa, smiled, and said, "Have a nice day."

It only took Samuel a few minutes to find his room. He opened the door to his suite and was stunned. *Truly beautiful,* he thought as he looked around. The hotel had spared no expense for his visit. There was even a personal buffet in the room. He leaned closer to the buffet, and the smell of fresh fruit instantly captured his senses. He peeked over to the right of the table and saw a few bottles of chilled champagne. *Perfect!* He uncorked one of the bottles and poured himself a glass. *This is the life.*

Samuel pulled a greeting card out of his suitcase. *A true fan*, he thought as he admired the shiny exterior design. On the front of the card there was a white and black spotted bear wearing a doctor's coat. He was sitting in front of a rack of cadavers with a questioning look on his face. The animal was holding a bottle of pills in one paw and a clear syringe in his other. The caption block above the bear read, "Have you missed your appointment lately?" Samuel opened the card and smiled when he saw the red writing. It said, "Don't worry, I have the right prescription for you!" The card was strangely signed, "A friend from the past." A small, round, yellow smiley face sticker in the bottom right-hand corner caught his eye. *I wonder who this is from.* He closed the card and placed it upright on the desk, next to the phone.

Samuel grabbed the morning newspaper from the table by the front door and sat down on a comfortable recliner chair. He opened the paper and scanned the headlines. One caught his attention, so he read the article.

> Marcona Police are investigating a mutilated body found inside a parked vehicle. The woman has been identified as twenty-five-year-old Shauna Holden. Police officials declined to release details of the murder but say the investigation is progressing."

Samuel shook his head. *What is this world coming to?* He grabbed his glass of champagne and took a few bites from the buffet. In a few days, he would do the presentation. Then it would be time for an extended vacation. *I'm long overdue for a vacation,* he thought. He glanced at the greeting card. *Maybe the unidentified sender will make himself or herself known.* The well-regarded physician wasn't aware that he was playing a role in devising his own demise.

# Chapter 13

# The Perfect Purchase

 Lucas cut out the newspaper story about Shauna and pinned it to an open space on his wall. *Time to close the book on Shauna Holden*, he thought as he shut the glass cabinet.

Organization and preparation were important to Lucas. "Sloppiness gets you caught," he muttered. He sat down at his tidy workbench, pulled in his chair, and sat straight up. Lucas had impeccable posture. He lifted the lid off a small metal box, reached inside, and carefully removed a rolled-up cloth blanket that was secured with a rope. The rope was worn and frayed. *I need to replace that.* He grabbed his knife and severed the rope in half with one quick stroke of the blade. The blanket sprung open, revealing twenty-four individual pockets. He unsnapped twelve of the pockets and removed a plastic syringe from each one. He inspected the syringes for damage. Once he was satisfied that they were free from defects, he set them aside. Then he reached under the table and grabbed a medium-size, black duffel bag. He unzipped it and sorted through several items until he found what he was looking for. Cautiously, he reached into the bag and withdrew a silver container. It was about two feet long and looked a lot like a thermos. The words, My Creation, were painted in red block letters on the top and bottom of the container." Lucas unscrewed the cap and removed the safety mechanism. He picked up the first syringe and filled it with a calculated amount of liquid from the silver container. He repeated the process with the other eleven syringes. When he was finished, he placed the filled syringes inside a backpack, and then placed the backpack inside the refrigerator. He knocked on the fridge and said, "Samuel's special surprise."

A feeling of giddiness came upon him. He chuckled. Then he laughed a little. Then he went completely against his norm and allowed the feeling to take over. He roared with laughter. A good five minutes went by before he took control of himself. He went from a laughing fit to a stern grimace in a split second. There was nothing gradual about it.

Lucas cleaned up his work area and headed upstairs. He turned on his desktop computer and did a search for an item that he needed. After a few minutes, he found what he was looking for. One store near him had it in stock. He wrote the store's address on a piece of scratch paper and headed out.

Lucas entered the store and approached a middle-aged clerk who was bending down arranging various fish food.

"Hello, can you help me?" Lucas asked him.

The man stood up and quickly dusted off his pants. "Sure, son, what do you need?"

Lucas held out a piece of scratch paper for the man to look at and said, "I would like to purchase this."

"Let's see what you have." The man leaned forward and looked at the design on the paper. "Hmm, I think we have that one over there." He pointed to a shelf across the room.

Lucas followed the man over to the shelf.

"Thanks, I have been looking for this type for a while," Lucas said.

The clerk chuckled. "Blue Skies Fish Emporium has everything, Sir."

Lucas shook his head in agreement. "It appears so."

"Sir, how many fish are you going to keep in it?"

"Just one, if everything works out," Lucas said as he ran his hand over the smooth glass.

"Fish get pretty lonely in a tank like that."

Lucas flashed a devious grin. "This one won't." He picked up the rectangular tank. "This is the twenty-five gallon model, isn't it?"

"Indeed it is."

"Great! Thanks again."

Lucas checked out at the self-service checkout lane, carried the tank out to the car, and stashed it in the trunk. He planned to fill the tank with his murky liquid concoction and let it sit overnight. He was making Samuel Longnecker's final resting place. *This is the perfect purchase for my plan.*

Lucas checked his watch. In twelve hours the Pleasure Cove's manager would be opening the club. A little smile creased Lucas' lips. *One more loose end to tie up. Just one more.*

# Chapter 14

# In the Right Direction

Kelli Jordan woke up late that morning. She was supposed to meet with Gloria Stephens the night before. When the woman never showed up at the hospital, Kelli and her partner decided to try it again in the morning. Craig backed out of the morning interview because he had to meet with the magistrate to get a warrant for the Pleasure Cove's security tapes.

Kelli parked along the curb in front of Gloria Stephen's charming, one-story residence. She walked up the cobblestone path and pushed the doorbell. A petite, silver-haired woman opened the door.

"Hello, you must be Detective Jordan," the woman said.

"Yes, Mrs. Stephens, I am. Sorry you couldn't make it last night."

"I couldn't stomach talking to anyone. Just wasn't ready."

"I understand," Kelli said in a consoling tone of voice.

"Oh, where are my manners?" Gloria stepped aside and motioned for Kelli to enter. "Come in. My head's still not all the way here. I shouldn't have let you stand in the cold like that."

Kelli smiled. "Not a problem. You okay to talk now?"

Gloria nodded her head. "Yes, Detective. I can talk. I'm sorry. I know it was a shock to everyone. I have never known anyone who has been murdered."

*Lucky you.* "I won't keep you long. Just a few questions," Kelli said.

Gloria led Kelli through a cramped hallway and opened the door to their right. The brightness from the lighting caused Kelli to shield her eyes.

"Sorry." Gloria pushed a silver button on the wall. The window shades rotated, making the room bearable.

Kelli glanced around the room as she walked through the door. The marble table and matching chairs were gorgeous. She detected the distinct fragrance of lilac. She inhaled through her nose. *Yep, that's definitely lilac.* The scent made the home feel relaxing and inviting.

Gloria pulled out a chair and motioned for Kelli to sit.

"I do appreciate your hospitality, Mrs. Stephens." Kelli plucked a file from her briefcase. "Like I said before, just a few questions for you."

Gloria put a thin silver cup in front of Kelli. "No worries. Cup of tea for you, Detective?"

"You didn't have to do that."

"Morning tea is my Achilles' heel." Gloria laughed.

Kelli smiled and thought, *A morning cigarette is mine*, but she kept that to herself and said, "It's always something, isn't it?" She took a sip of tea.

"Yes, it is."

"Mrs. Stephens, how long had Shauna been working at

the hospital?"

"About a year."

Kelli grabbed her notebook and pen. "Did she have any problems at work with other employees?"

"No more than the average person," Gloria said as she played with the cup in front of her. "Most of the employees didn't really talk to her very often."

"You mean they didn't get along with her?" Kelli asked.

"No, it wasn't that. She was a straightforward girl. She came to work, did her job, and left.

"So she didn't hang out with people at work?" Kelli wrote down a few notes.

"Not that I ever saw. It seemed to me that Shauna was a very private person. More so than most."

*If you only knew*, Kelli thought. "Did Shauna spend time with anyone at all?"

"If she did, I never saw it."

"So, Shauna just pretty much came to work, did her job, and left?"

"For the most part, yes, that really was it," Gloria shrugged her shoulders.

"Okay, how about any altercations with staff, patients, or anyone else?

"Detective, I never witnessed any problems such as that. I don't even think the girl had a steady male friend." Gloria's face turned a dark shade of red. "I didn't mean anything—"

"—I understand." Kelli shifted in her seat and shuffled a few papers. "Tell me about the night she died."

"I received a call that a patient had passed away. There

wasn't anyone to take the body to the morgue."

"So you chose Shauna?"

Gloria folded her arms across her chest. "We were short on staff and . . . yes, she was available."

"I see."

"About five minutes after Shauna left to take care of the body, I received a call from someone in the morgue."

"Someone?" Kelli raised her eyebrows.

"Yes. I think the attendant's name was Patrick. He said Shauna was there and he was helping her."

Kelli flipped through several pages of employee names, searching for the one Gloria had just given her. "Are you sure his name was Patrick?"

"Yes, that's what he said."

"Did you recognize his voice?"

"No. I know the morgue has several people on staff, so I don't think I know him." Gloria looked perplexed.

"What did his voice sound like?"

"Very deep—almost sexy, even." Gloria blushed.

"Gloria, I don't see anyone named Patrick listed on the employee listing in my folder here." Kelli thumbed through the listing a second time.

"I'm sure that's what he told me," Gloria said.

"Maybe human resources missed a name on here," Kelli said. She wrote herself a reminder note to check with human resources again. "Okay, after the call, what happened?"

"A few minutes later, I got another call. It was Shauna. She said nobody was in the morgue." A worried expression came over Gloria's face. Recounting the story made her see the phone call in a different light, and it suddenly hit her that she had blown Shauna off without a second thought. "Oh no," Gloria said. She covered her mouth with both hands and stared blankly as she thought, *I didn't know Shauna was in danger. If I had paid more attention, maybe she would still be here.*

"Gloria, stay with me here. What did you tell Shauna when she told you no one was there?"

Gloria's face turned ashen. "I told her that I spoke with the attendant and that she would be fine." She let out an angry, desperate grunt and swatted the expensive glass off the table.

"You didn't know, Gloria." Kelli moved to the chair that was right next to the woman.

"I didn't even think." Gloria covered her face.

"Nobody is going to blame you. Someone knew she was coming downstairs." Kelli said in an attempt to comfort Gloria. "How long was she gone before anyone realized?"

"Maybe twenty minutes." Gloria sobbed.

"That's good. It helps us set up a timeline." Kelli patted Gloria on the shoulder.

Comforting people wasn't Kelli's strong suit. The military taught Kelli to be strong in bad situations. Emotional outbursts, like the one Gloria was exhibiting, had not been a part of Kelli's life since high school.

"Your information may help us catch him," Kelli said. A weak smile crossed her face.

"I don't know why someone would want to kill Shauna." Gloria grasped Kelli's hand tightly.

"We are going to find out, Gloria." Kelli's knuckles were

turning white from Gloria's strong grip.

Kelli thanked Gloria and gave her the number to a grief counselor that the department assigned to violent cases such as murder. Then she returned to her car and lit a cigarette. *Ahh, that's better.* Kelli sat on the hood of her car while she smoked and thought about the facts of the case. *The mystery morgue attendant is the key. There's no doubt about it. I will scour the hospital personnel files, but I'm not going to hold my breath. I don't think the mystery man was an employee. At least I have a timeline now. That's something I didn't have before.*

# Chapter 15

# Loose Ends

Lucas stood in front of the wall-length mirror and admired his professional appearance. He picked up the brown, leather paddle-gun holster, laced it through the matching belt, and adjusted it so he could easily grab the weapon with his right hand. He slipped on the navy suit coat and left it unbuttoned. *What a disguise*, he thought. He grabbed one of the two plastic bags on the workbench, fished out the green memo notebook, and placed it in his upper left breast pocket, along with a sleek, red ballpoint pen. He removed a thin strip of hair from the other bag, attached it above his lip, and smoothed it out until he was satisfied. *One more thing and then my disguise is complete.* He opened the glass cabinet and searched through a drawer until he found the polished shield. "Ah, Detective Alex Barnum, again you are an asset in helping me with my masterpieces," Lucas said aloud as he clipped the shield to the worn holder and stuck it on his leather belt, opposite of his weapon. One quick glance in the mirror and he knew it was time.

Lucas went through the back door to the garage. He removed the dusty car cover, exposing an early 1990s model red Honda Accord. "Seems like old times girl," Lucas said as he neatly folded up the cover. The red Honda had been his safe haven for getting to one deadly location to another. *I really did like the sport utility, but everything good comes to an end.* He opened the trunk. A worn, green, wool blanket with the initials BHA sewn on it caught his attention. *I should have burned that thing*, he thought.

Looking at the blanket instantly brought back memories of failure, botched medical experiments, the loss of many test subjects, and the loss of his career. Lucas couldn't get over the unfairness of being punished while Samuel's career thrived. *Samuel, you may have been exonerated of your culpability, but you are going to have a day in court—Lucas' Court of Death.*

Lucas slammed the trunk shut and took a few deep breaths. He had to be on top of his game. He was quite aware that one slip-up would ruin everything. He reached for the keys above the visor and started the car. The steady sound of the smooth engine soothed his tension. He pushed the button on the garage door opener and eased the car into traffic.

Grant Nesmith stripped off his gray trench coat and brushed off the remaining snow from his clothes. Then he flipped on Pleasure Cove's interior lights, headed up the stairs, and waved his key card in front of the reader to gain access to his office. He still couldn't believe that Shauna/Jade had been murdered in the parking lot.

Grant sat down at his desk and discovered the answering machine had two messages. He listened to the first and erased it. He pushed a button to put the phone on speaker and let the next message play. The metallic sound of a man's voice reverberated out from the miniature speaker.

"Mr. Nesmith, this is Detective Berte from the Marcona Police Department. I am calling to inform you, Sir, that the police department is obtaining an order to review Pleasure Cove's video records in regards to a murder investigation. The department expects to have confirmation by mid-day, and we want you to be present when we arrive. If you have any questions, feel free to contact me or Detective Kelli Jordan at the police department. Thank you for your cooperation."

Grant erased the message. *Just fucking great,* he thought. *The club doesn't need this kind of publicity. The city council has been trying to close Pleasure Cove forever. This will be just another bullet in a smoking gun to do just that.*

Grant reached into the middle drawer of his desk and pulled out a small silver key on a chain. He walked over to a wall print of a gold hair beauty named Vanna Vixen. She was the Pleasure Cove's first headliner and had been instrumental in making the place a success. He inserted the key into the keyhole, turned it, and the wall print popped open, revealing a DVR system along with several other pieces of recording equipment. In the lower right corner, there were many disc cases labeled with various names of past performers. He sorted through a few until he grabbed the case labeled, Jade Blue Omega Star. It contained the disc footage of Jade's last performance. He locked the wall print back into place and set the case on his desk. *Might as well have it ready,* he figured.

Grant decided to review the security footage, just so he knew what was on it. He popped the disc out of the case and walked over to the high-definition television display. He slid the disc into the open slot. The security system recorded on a 24-hour loop and timestamped the footage on the discs, so he fast forwarded to the appropriate time. About a quarter of the way through, he found Jade's performance. He hit play and watched Jade perform. At one point, a muscular man approached the stage and tossed something next to Jade. The man stepped out of the camera's view not long afterwards. Jade picked up the item after her performance. Grant couldn't tell what the item was. *Probably just money,* he thought. He continued watching until she stepped off the stage. He didn't notice anything ominous or threatening in the footage. *There's nothing on here.* He removed the disc from the player and put it back into the case on top of his desk.

Grant was about to check the bar order for the evening when he heard a buzzing sound coming from the building's back door entry. *Early for any deliveries,* he thought as he descended the rear stairs. He peered out the peephole. It looked like someone was holding a gold badge in front of the small window. Grant glanced down at his watch and frowned. He hit the intercom.

"Yes, I thought you guys said noon," Grant said.

"Sir, I'm Detective Barnum with Marcona Police," Lucas said.

"I thought the other two were coming." Grant felt uneasy.

He tried to reason with himself, thinking, *The officer does have a badge.*

"Sir, the others should be here shortly. I'm just a little early."

"All right. Give me a second." Grant slid the two locking devices off the hinges and opened the door to greet his visitor.

# Chapter 16

# Recovering His Evidence

Lucas watched the door open and then stepped inside Pleasure Cove. He took note of Grant's slender frame and well-dressed appearance.

"I just got a call from Detective Berte. Like I said before, I thought you all were showing up at noon," Grant said as he shut the door.

Lucas peeked at his watch. *Looks like I have a little time to get acquainted*, he thought. Then he looked at Grant and said, "I'm the senior investigator for this homicide. I have been out of the area. Headed over here first thing today."

"Oh, I thought it was the female and that man who were in charge." Grant stopped at the bar and grabbed a bottle of Scotch. "Would you like a drink?"

Lucas waved him off. "Can't stand the stuff." He smiled. *This is going to be easy.* "Sir, do you have the security tape ready to go?"

Grant eyed the man with suspicion as he poured himself an alcoholic beverage. "In my office. It's a DVD, not a tape, Detective," Grant said smartly.

"Right, all this new tech stuff gets me confused," Lucas

played along. He knew exactly what security devices were in place. He tapped the counter. "I'll take that drink, if you are still offering?"

Grant nodded his head. "I'm glad you reconsidered."

"I'm not going to be doing too much driving. Don't tell on me." Lucas snickered.

"Ha! That's the last thing I will do," Grant joked. Then he handed the officer a drink.

Lucas took a sip of Scotch. "The security DVD, if you please."

"I should make you guys wait until I see the order from the judge, but there's nothing really too revealing on it anyway." Grant pointed up the stairwell.

"Really, nothing at all?" Lucas asked. He followed Grant up the stairs to his office. *Maybe I don't need to kill this man, after all.* He watched Grant use the key card. *No, I will kill him.*

Grant pulled out a chair and said, "Go ahead and take a seat. I will get the DVD for you."

"Thank you." Lucas gawked as Grant opened the wall print. "Nice hiding place."

"Safest place I could think of."

Lucas noticed a black case on the desk. He read the date written on it and realized it was the DVD he'd come for. He didn't say anything, but he paid close attention as Grant fumbled around with two other cases that matched the one on the desk. *Sly bastard. He's trying to trick me*, Lucas thought.

"Yes, I guess that is the best place to hide the recording system," Lucas said. He slowly lifted the firearm from his holster while he kept a close eye on Grant.

Grant returned to the desk, sat down, and slid one of the cases in the officer's direction. "There you go. Nothing great on there."

Lucas picked up the DVD and looked at the date. *Nice try.* The ink on the label was smudged. Lucas knew it was a fake.

"I don't know why you would give me the wrong DVD," Lucas said. He thrust out the weapon from its hiding place and aimed it at Grant's chest. "Now, why would you—"

"—Detective, I don't think you have the right—"

"—The one on the desk." Lucas tapped the table with his fist. Tell me what DVD that is." Lucas moved closer and forced the steel muzzle into Grant's chest.

"What the fuck! Why pull a gun?" Grant's fear turned to anger.

"Because maybe I'm not a cop." Lucas reached into his right coat pocket and removed a small, black piece of hollow metal. "Do you know what this is?"

"Hey, come on. You can't kill me. I haven't done anything."

Grant leaned away from the gun, but the man stayed his course and forced the barrel against him.

"Really, I haven't lied to you," Grant said. His fear returned full-force.

"This is where you tell the truth." Lucas removed the gun just long enough to attach the silencer. "Where is a pen and paper?" Lucas backed the gun off.

"It's in . . . the bottom drawer," Grant responded.

"Get it," Lucas ordered.

Grant's hands were trembling so much that it took him a

few moments to open his desk drawer and grab a pen and paper. He pushed the items toward Lucas.

"Here you go. Don't kill me," Grant begged.

"Here is what you are going to do. I want you to write down exactly what I say. Do you understand?"

"Yes . . . I do." A tear ran down the right side of Grant's face.

"Maybe, if you follow directions, I will let you go." Lucas smiled. He wanted to give the pathetic club manager a little hope.

Lucas recited several lines. Grant began writing, but then he stopped and tried to fight. Lucas placed the gun between Grant's eyes, quickly ending the confrontation. After that, Grant completed the letter without causing another stir.

"Are you going to let me go now?" Grant asked hopefully, even though he knew he wasn't getting out of there.

Lucas studied the words on the paper and was very pleased with the results. He removed the silencer from the gun and placed it back inside the holster. He knelt down by his captive.

"You did well, but I'm sorry to say, just not good enough to stay alive."

Lucas swiftly withdrew the small syringe from his pocket and thrust it into Grant's larynx. It happened so fast that Grant didn't have a chance to fight back. The drug quickly coursed through his veins. Joyfully, Lucas watched him drop to the ground and gasp for air. Grant's body became completely paralyzed, including his chest. He was suffocating but couldn't inhale to get the oxygen he desperately needed to stay alive.

Gurgling sounds came from his mouth as the last of the air escaped his lungs.

Lucas pulled a pair of white latex gloves out of his front pants pocket and slipped them on his hands. Without much effort, he picked up Grant's body and sat it back on the chair. Then he lifted his own pant leg and removed a small six-round handgun from his ankle holster. He placed the gun in Grant's right hand. Then he wrapped his own hand around Grant's and grasped firmly, forcing the dead man's fingers to wrap around the weapon. With the flick of a finger, he slid Grant's forefinger over the trigger. He placed the end of the gun barrel against Grant's head, put his own finger on top of Grant's forefinger, and pulled the trigger. The sound of the gunshot filled the office. Then there was nothing but silence. *Not the best way to go*, Lucas thought.

Lucas snatched the disc from Grant's desk and left the note in its place before heading for the exit. He opened the door and looked back over his shoulder to catch one last glimpse of his work. *Absolutely wonderful*, he thought. He reached up and rubbed the heart necklace and smiled. At that moment, he truly felt untouchable.

# Chapter 17

# Following a Lead

Detective Kelli Jordan returned to the hospital to follow up on the information Gloria Stephens had given her. She was hoping to get a lead on the mysterious morgue attendant. She stepped off the elevator on the administrative floor, walked down the hallway, and entered the human resources department office. There were three cubicles, each occupied by an employee. All of them appeared to be busy. None of them bothered to engage the investigator when she entered the room.

*Nice,* Kelli thought. *Time to get their attention.* She flashed her badge, cleared her throat loudly, and said, "Hello, I'm looking for Susan Ibanez."

An attractive latino woman in her early twenties popped her head out of a cubicle, smiled, and said, "Hi, I'm Susan. Give me a second."

A few minutes later, Susan strolled up to the counter. "How may I help you, Officer?"

"Actually, it's Detective. I need to check your employee roster for a possible suspect in a homicide."

"I'm sorry . . . Detective . . . do you know the name of the person you're looking for?" Susan reached under the counter and produced a large blue binder.

"I have a first name. That's all I could get.

Susan chuckled as she opened the book. "What is the name?"

"It's Patrick. Well, sorry, that was the name he gave my witness." Kelli shrugged her shoulders.

"Okay. Do you know which department this Patrick person works for?"

"The subject was down in the morgue when he called the witness," Kelli said.

"The listing I have here is alphabetized by the last names, and it doesn't separate employees by department. Let me see if I can pull up the employee database on my computer. It would be easier and quicker to do an electronic name search and pull up a department employee list rather than read through a list of the entire hospital staff." Susan closed the binder.

"That would be great." Kelli could only hope the mystery man was somewhere in those records.

"I can't promise anything," Susan warned as she escorted Kelli to the far cubicle.

"Well, anything you can do will be appreciated." Kelli pulled up a chair.

Susan sat down in front of the computer and tried to access the employee database. Within one minute, a list of names appeared on the screen. She scrolled through a few of the pages of names, and then, after a few mouse clicks, the morgue roster appeared.

Susan looked at Kelli and pointed at the computer monitor. "Here are the employees that work in the morgue." She turned toward the monitor, looked at the names, and stuck her finger next to one listing. She held her finger in place as she looked back at Kelli. "I have one Patrick on file. Mr. Patrick Ezine. He's a part-timer. He only works weekends." She dropped her hand and turned to the computer. "I'm printing out the list of morgue employees for you." She hit the print command. A few seconds later the pages appeared in her printer tray. She grabbed the printed list and handed it to Kelli.

"Do you know when he worked last?" Kelli asked, hoping she had found the break they needed in the case.

"Let me check." She tapped a few keys on the keyboard. "The last shift he worked here was three months ago. Usually after ninety days, an employee is let go. So it looks like he will be off the books soon." Susan tapped a few more keys. "No paycheck issued to him since then."

"Do you have his current address?" Kelli asked. She knew Susan had already broken protocol to help her, but she really wanted to solve the case, so she continued pushing for more information.

"I will print it out for you." Susan pulled up Patrick's address and hit the print command. "Detective, I do have something to ask you." She grabbed the printed address out of the printer tray and handed it to Kelli.

Kelli stuffed the paper into her folder as she replied, "What kind of question?"

Susan's face became a little flushed as she whispered, "The newspaper said she was a stripper. Is that true?"

"Ms. Ibanez, we all have our secrets. Ms. Holden had a major one. I think it got her killed."

Susan nodded. "If you need anything else, let me know."

"I will. You have given me an important piece of the puzzle." Kelli shook the woman's hand.

Anxious to speak with the newly identified man, Kelli quickly headed out of the hospital and slid into the driver's seat of her patrol car. She looked down at the paper Susan had given her to find the man's address. *1212 Conger Street. That is on the other side of town, and I'm due to meet Craig in less than thirty minutes.* Her cell phone chirped. She looked at the caller ID, saw that it was Craig, and answered the phone.

"Hey, I was just thinking about you," Kelli said.

"Kelli, you aren't gonna believe this. I'm on my way back to the strip club."

"You got the subpoena for the records already?"

"Not exactly. There has been another death. This time inside the club. Head that way please," Craig urged.

*You gotta be shitting me.* "Another stripper?" Kelli asked.

"No, it's the manager, Grant Nesmith. Emergency dispatch got a call from one of the girls who found him."

"What the fuck?" *Who would go after him?*

"There is a note at the scene."

"A note? You mean a suicide note?"

"I wish that were true. I will be there in ten," Craig said.

"See you there."

Kelli hung up the phone and thought about the latest event in the case. *In a few day timespan, two people have turned* up dead at the same location. Out of a fear of getting caught, most killers wouldn't dare venture into the same waters twice. Whoever is responsible for these murders isn't the least worried about it at all.

# Chapter 18

# Suicide or Homicide?

Kelli Jordan sped into Pleasure Cove's parking lot. The compilation of various news station reporters and their ensemble of equipment took up a front row seat. Two murders in less than a week in Marcona was almost unheard of, and having them both in the same place was, without question, the hot topic of the hour. Kelli looked around at all the people and thought, *What a media frenzy!* As she got out of the car, several reporters rushed her with their microphones poised to capture every juicy detail.

A blonde woman working for a national news affiliate flashed her press pass at Kelli and asked, "Detective, is the man who killed the girl a victim himself?"

Kelli was confused. She raised her hand and said, "I'm unaware of anything right now."

A male reporter dressed to the nines—and the epitome of sleazy—pushed a few of his brethren journalists aside and positioned himself in front of Kelli.

*Oh shit. Not this asshole*, Kelli thought.

"Ron Plesic from Seventeen News. Is it true that this man had a sexual relationship with the previous victim.

*Ron fucking Plesic.* "Gimme a break. Where did you get that, Mr. Plesic?"

Kelli waved to a uniformed officer and pointed out the sleazy reporter in front of her. As the officer attempted to break up the mob, Kelli pushed her way to the back door of the club where a female officer stood guard.

Kelli flashed her badge at the guard and asked, "Where is Detective Berte?"

"Ma'am, he is on the second floor."

Kelli climbed the stairs and entered Grant Nesmith's office. The interior was filled with a mix of crime scene analysts and plainclothes investigators. Craig was perched over Grant's body, snapping a few photos. Kelli walked up to Craig, slipped on a pair of latex gloves, and knelt next to him.

"What a fucking mess out there," Kelli said. "Looks like there's more reporters than there are cops."

"Did you see that Ron Sleazic asshole?" Craig asked.

"Yes. That piece of shit is already stirring the pot. So what do we have here?"

"Single gunshot wound to the head." Craig positioned the body so Kelli could see the wound. Then he pointed out the silver handgun on the floor. "That's definitely a .380. The serial numbers are scratched off."

"Figures." Kelli looked at the cabinet immediately to the left of the deceased and thought, *The blood pattern looks awkward.* "Craig, look at this." She pointed at the cabinet. "Not too much blood on here."

"Yeah, but take a look at the note he left. It's in the evidence bag, at the top."

Kelli grabbed the note out of the evidence bag and read it.

> I'm responsible for the murder of my former lover, Shauna Holden. She was my complete world, and I can't go on living this shallow existence of a pathetic life. I am truly sorry for my actions and I hope people will be able to forgive me.
>
> Grant P. Nesmith

Kelli turned to her partner. "Do you believe this?" She set the plastic bag back on the desk.

"Love will do crazy things to a person." Craig shook his head. He finished collecting the evidence and handed it to one of the techs.

"Craig, not funny. It doesn't make sense."

"What doesn't make sense? The guy killed her. I don't see anything here saying otherwise."

"Hear me out for a sec. The girl was in her twenties. The late Mr. Nesmith was well into his forties."

"Maybe she enjoyed older men." Craig snapped several more photographs.

"Not a girl who looks like that." Kelli pointed to the wall print of Shauna Holden.

"I see where you're going with this, but I'm not biting."

"Craig, how do you explain the paralytic drug in the girl's bloodstream?"

"I don't know. Maybe he knew somebody who could get the stuff for him."

"Even if that were the case, how did he get in the back of the hospital? Remember the key card?"

"Kelli, she worked there. It's possible she gave it to him."

"Let's get a warrant for his house. If he fucking did this, the key card and her implants should be there somewhere."

"Already ahead of you on that. Should have it within the hour," Craig said.

"Bear with me here. Nesmith and the girl are an item. Something happens and he kills her. Then this guy kills himself because he feels guilty about it. He even leaves a note. It's too cliché," Kelli mocked.

"It may be cliché, but it fits." Craig turned and looked at Kelli. "What do you think is going on?"

"Why would the serial numbers be scratched off the gun if it was his?" Kelli asked.

"Easy enough. The guy bought it off the street. He didn't want to get caught with it."

Kelli dismissed his response. "I was just at the hospital, and I think we have a suspect. Maybe a temp employee there."

"We have a confession from Nesmith." Craig motioned in the dead man's direction.

"I just have a hunch on this." Kelli scanned the room in search for more evidence. "I also have the nursing supervisor telling us that someone was down in the morgue that night. I think he could be our guy."

"Okay, if this hunch of yours is right, then why would Nesmith admit to a murder he didn't do?" Craig inspected the area adjacent to the body.

"I don't know that answer, but I would feel better if we knew that he doesn't have any of that paralytic drug in his system."

"His head has a hole in it. I can see that's what killed him." Craig pointed at the quarter-sized wound in Nesmith's skull.

"Humor me. Call the medical examiner and see if I'm right," Kelli pleaded.

"I'll give him a call, but he's going to think we're crazy, especially with a fucking suicide note."

Kelli stared at Craig, frustrated, as she thought about the case. *This is just too perfect. There is no way Grant Nesmith was having sex with Shauna Holden. I think the man in the morgue had something to do with both murders, even if he didn't kill either of them. Suicide or homicide is the question I need answered. When the medical examiner completes the blood work on Grant Nesmith, I will have the answer.*

# Chapter 19

# Into the Fire

Lucas inserted the DVD into the player and hit play. He wanted to make sure it was the one that showed him approaching the stripper. The footage started off grainy. Within seconds, it cleared up. The camera loop appeared to be on a twenty-four hour rotation, starting at 0600 hours. Lucas fast forwarded until he saw himself appear on the screen. *Excellent, it will be difficult to prove I was there without the evidence*, he thought. He removed the DVD from the player, put it back in the case, and placed it into the plastic bag that contained the DVD footage of him in the police officer uniform.

The news program playing on the television caught Lucas' attention. He looked at the TV screen and almost laughed. A local news reporter was standing in the Pleasure Cove parking lot, giving a play by play of the events. Lucas picked up the remote and turned up the volume.

"In the last several hours, police officials have continued their investigation into the apparent suicide of a man at this location. According to our sources, the deceased woman found in the parking lot a few days ago may have relevance in this case. To recap what happened, at approximately 10:30 a.m. this morning, police officials were notified that a man was found dead. The cause of death appears to be a self-inflicted gunshot wound. The identity of the man is being withheld until his family is notified. We will have more on this story as it develops. For Seventeen News, this is Ron Plesic reporting."

*Always too easy,* Lucas thought. He turned off the TV and stuffed the bag containing the DVD's into the inside pocket of his winter coat. He chuckled. *The pathetic police have nothing.* He grabbed the garage door opener on his way out the back door and headed for the detached garage.

Lucas entered the garage and closed the door behind himself. He dropped the bag of DVD's into a rusted burn barrel and doused it with lighter fluid. Then he lit a match and tossed it into the barrel. Dark smoke soon filled the garage. He hit the button on the garage door opener. Frigid air swept inside, causing him to shiver. He watched the flames melt the evidence into nothingness. *No worries now. After I deal with Samuel, I will slip into the darkness once again.*

Lucas was disappointed he wouldn't be able to retrieve the fifty-cent piece from Brian Jeffers. *I really don't know how incompetent Ronald Trapp managed to get the upper hand on Jeffers and his police staff. That was a true pity, but life goes on. Tomorrow I will visit the hotel where Samuel is staying and begin the preparations for my next masterpiece.* A surge of adrenalin pulsed through Lucas' body, making his heart skip a beat. Revenge never felt so good.

# Chapter 20

# Recovery Is Not a Luxury

Desoto Valley Police Chief Brian Jeffers pushed open the door to his home. *Just like I left it. Not as messy, though.* The doctor allowed Brian to leave the hospital after only a couple of days, but he was insistent he get his much needed rest. He warned Brian that if he didn't rest, it would be a short reprieve, and he would have to return to the hospital and stay until he was 100-percent healthy.

When Brian was in the hospital, he decided to relocate his daughters to a place he knew was safe. He had little family left, so his mother-in-law in Nebraska was the only option. With the kids gone, the house was uncomfortably quiet.

Brian set his small suitcase on the floor, which caused a sharp pain to shoot through his chest. He rubbed the spot where the bullet had torn through his flesh. *Ronald Trapp killed three of my officers, and the bastard escaped. Why did he come here? It was risky, even for a heinous kidnapper turned murderer.* He winced as he reached into his jeans pocket and pulled out a bottle of pain killers. He unscrewed the lid, took out two pills, popped them into his mouth, and swallowed. The welcome, yet temporary, relief from pain would soon hit. He thought about his friend, the Mayor of Desoto Valley, telling him to take his time healing before he even thought about working. Against the mayor's and the doctor's wishes, Brian planned to spend most of his time off finding out why Ronald Trapp had followed him to Desoto. *Most criminals with his type of record would try to avoid police altogether.*

Brian pushed the door to his home office open and was greeted by the unpacked boxes. So much had gone on that he almost forgot the move was barely complete. He gingerly sat down at the desk, turned on his computer, and flipped through his silver Rolodex. *There it is.* He activated the hands free option on the phone and dialed.

"Valentine Police Department. This is Cynthia Cornerstone speaking."

Brian smiled. *Her voice is still as smooth as it always was.* Cynthia was his former administrative assistant and one of his only remaining friends. He was sure she had heard about the shooting.

"Cynthia, my one true love, it's Brian."

"Oh my, Brian, I'm so glad to hear from you. We just heard last night about what happened. Chief sent some flowers for you—"

"—Cynthia, I know better," Brian scolded.

"Okay, I sent them, dear. How are you doing?" Cynthia asked with sincerity.

"I got hit twice. Only one round went through the vest." Brian unconsciously rubbed his chest.

Cynthia hesitated. "Lucky to be alive, dear. We have been

looking for Ronald Trapp for months. Now he shows up on your doorstep."

"Lucky me," Brian joked. "Cynthia, I will be working from home, and I can use your help."

"Anything for you, Brian. Chief really misses you here, but he would never say it. You know those masculine types." Cynthia laughed.

Brian could always count on Cynthia to cheer him up when he was in bad spirits.

"Of course I do. Is the aforementioned one in?"

"Indeed he is. I will transfer the call. Brian, I'm glad you're okay. Those beautiful daughters of yours couldn't handle losing both parents," Cynthia said with a somber tone to her voice.

"Thanks. I wonder everyday if things would have turned out different—"

"—Not your fault, young man. You need to remember that."

Cynthia transferred the call. The consoling Cynthia was soon replaced with the gruff voice of Valentine Police Chief Ralph Anderson.

"Chief Brian Jeffers, it's good to hear from you," Chief Ralph Anderson said in his official spokesman's tone.

"Hey Ralph, it sounds like you are still indulging in those cigars," Brian joked.

"Ha! Of course. That has always been a weakness of mine. Think of it this way—I will have a great job in radio after I retire."

"Touché. I'm glad you're thinking ahead."

"Always, my boy." Ralph softened his voice. "On a serious

note, I'm happy you're doing better."

"You and me both. It doesn't make a lot of sense for Trapp to be here."

"I was thinking the same thing. I have a few undercover officers putting feelers out there to find out why," Ralph said.

"Appreciate it. Has he been active there in town?" Brian asked.

"Nothing on the radar here. The last I heard, he was wanted for questioning regarding a murdered teenager on the other side of the state."

"Probably one of his high school drug dealers," Brian said, stating the obvious. He reached for his computer mouse and double clicked on a folder labeled, INVESTIGATIONS. A window opened up with a bunch of sub-folders in it.

"Yes, that's been the general consensus. Trapp seemed to have disappeared after—"

Brian cut Ralph off mid-sentence. "—And made his way my direction." He double clicked on one of the sub-folders and typed a few sentences.

"Hold on a sec, Brian. Cynthia just walked in here and handed me some information."

Brian heard paper shuffling in the background.

"This is interesting, to say the least." Ralph whistled.

Interesting? "Share with the class," Brian said.

"Appears two of Trapp's associates were found dead last week. It says the location was a warehouse in Marcona, North Dakota."

"That's not even close to here. I only noticed his car outside the police department for a couple of days."

"When was that?" Ralph asked.

"The day before the shooting." Brian typed in some more information. "The report in front of me says the bodies were found last Thursday," Ralph added.

"So he kills them, drives two states, and that leaves us where we are right now," Brian said.

"Seems that way," Ralph said.

"Could you fax me that info? I want to investigate this further, and it will be good therapy while I'm healing."

"Not a problem, but you probably should rest."

"Until I find that son of a bitch, I'm not going to be able to rest." Brian recited his fax number.

"Well don't go out and get yourself all shot up again. Keep me in the loop about what's going on."

"Don't worry. I won't get caught off-guard again."

"I don't think that was the case. You guys were outgunned. Be grateful you're walking around."

"I appreciate the sentiment. If he was watching me, I can't believe he was the brains of the whole thing." Brian closed the open folder on his computer.

"That is hard to believe. Son, if I can help, feel free to give us a call. I know Cynthia misses you around here."

"Will do. Thanks again!"

The phone line disconnected.

Brian was anxious to see the murder report for Trapp's two dirtbag friends. *I don't think Trapp can even tie his own shoes without being told. There has to be someone else pulling the two-bit killer's strings.* Brian resigned himself to the fact that someone had sent Ronald Trapp to kill him. He also believed that certain someone would no doubt be watching the local papers and media for confirmation of his death.

The perfect idea came to Brian. He hoped it would work. He flipped to a name in his address book and dialed the number on his phone.

# Chapter 21

# Proven Right

Kelli Jordan followed her partner through the front doors of the Marcona Police Department. Prior to their arrival, they had just finished wrapping up the crime scene at Pleasure Cove. The medical examiner's investigation was the final step. Kelli insisted to the medical examiner that the death of Nesmith was suspicious. She knew Craig wasn't happy that she shared her suspicions with the examiner. Most of the other officers agreed with Craig. The evidence wasn't in her favor, but she had a gut feeling that it was all too perfect. *The man kills Shauna Holden and then leaves a note taking responsibility? Just not right*, she thought. The usage of the paralytic drug was the main reason she couldn't process the case like everyone else.

Craig pushed the button on the elevator and glanced back at Kelli. "Not everything is a conspiracy," he teased.

"I didn't say it was a conspiracy. I just have the feeling that whoever did this . . . well . . . it wasn't Grant."

Craig remained silent as the two rode the elevator to the third floor where the homicide and robbery divisions shared a workspace. The homicide and robbery divisions were split up by approximately thirty cubicles. It was late, so there were only a few people working. Kelli went to her desk and booted up her laptop.

Craig entered Kelli's cubicle and said, "Kelli, I understand instincts, but the fact is that the angle the bullet exited the skull and the trajectory both point to suicide."

"I'll go to my original point. What about the paralytic drug? Where did he get that?" Kelli asked.

"That's a valid argument by itself, but not with the other evidence we found."

"Valid? I think it's the piece of evidence that matters. Do you remember what the medical examiner said when we found Shauna?" Kelli leaned forward.

"Of course I remember, but Grant Nesmith had gunpowder residue on his right hand. He fired the gun." Craig slid onto a chair next to Kelli.

"Maybe he didn't."

"What? You're kidding, right?" Craig shook his head.

"Listen, I know it sounds far-fetched, but what if someone else pulled the trigger?" Kelli turned her chair to face Craig. "Think about it. Who would suspect that?"

A disapproving frown formed on Craig's face. "Not even me. How much sleep have you had lately?"

"That has nothing to do with it. My point is that most people wouldn't suspect that."

"Absolutely right. Not any of the investigators who use the skills of deductive reasoning based on physical and trace evidence." Craig stood up to leave.

Kelli yanked on her desk drawer, pulled out the case file,

which was already open to a picture of Shauna Holden's corpse, and slammed it down on top of her desk. "Look at those cuts underneath each of her breasts. Do you actually believe the club guy could do shit that accurate?" Shauna's face turned red.

Craig turned back to her and snatched up several pictures. He gawked at the brutal photos. "I don't—"

Kelli continued her rant without waiting for Craig to finish speaking. "—I haven't seen anything in Nesmith's background that shows he possessed even the tiniest amount of medical knowledge."

"There was hardly any background on this guy through the criminal database. I will check again." Craig forced a smile.

"Tomorrow we should have a search warrant for Nesmith's house. If he really did this, the implants should be there," Kelli said.

"Yeah, maybe if we find the implants, it will convince you that Nesmith killed Shauna and then committed suicide." Craig turned and headed down the hall toward his own desk.

Kelli called after him. "Did the order come through on the club's security tapes?"

"Yes, Jacobs and Stinton will be bringing them in for us. They knew we were busy."

"Great. Maybe it will show us something. I also want to get in touch with that part-time morgue guy. He might have some answers for us."

"Gotcha." Craig disappeared into his cubicle.

Kelli put the case file back in her drawer and started typing her report on her meeting with Gloria Stephens. She was so focused on her work that she didn't hear Craig when he returned. His face was pale.

"Medical Examiner Kurt Delong left a message on my machine. There were traces of the paralytic drug in Grant Nesmith's bloodstream."

"I knew it," Kelli said with a confident look on her face.

"He wants us to go to his office." Craig turned and headed toward the elevator without saying another word.

Kelli quickly closed her laptop, stood up, and followed Craig.

Maybe Kelli should have taken solace in the fact that her theory on the paralytic drug was on the money, but overall, maybe being right should have frightened her even more.

# Chapter 22

# Lucas' Visit

Lucas parked the Honda in the sparsely filled lot. The twenty-four-hour diner was a good choice because of its proximity to Samuel Longnecker's hotel. He cracked open the door and felt the frigid air. Hastily, he got out of the car and removed his duffel bag from the trunk. He reached into the bag, removed a dark wool skullcap, and placed it snugly on his head. Then he scurried into the woods. As he trudged through the fresh snow, he glanced at the M2 compass, hoping the device was accurate. He pushed onward through the foliage, even though his legs felt heavy and his muscles were cramping. Finally, he reached a small clearing. He smiled when he noticed the red and green lights outlining the Jos Glades Hotel. He kept walking.

Lucas crept along the line of trees adjacent to the parking complex. *Not much traffic*, he thought. *The weather must have kept the majority of the hotel guests in for the evening.* He inched his way to the back service entrance. The steel door was propped open. Several employees were standing outside. It looked like they were taking a break. Lucas stepped into the light and walked up to the group.

"Hello, can you guys help me?" Lucas asked.

A sandy haired man in his early twenties responded, "Sir, this is the employee entrance. Are you lost or something?"

"I guess you could say that. I took a little walk and dropped my key card on the ground out there." Lucas pointed in the direction of the woods.

"Man, it's freezing. Why were you messing around in the woods?" the young man asked.

Lucas smiled. "Well, I was waiting for a woman."

"She must be freaky if she likes hanging out in this cold." The young man laughed.

"Maybe a little. Would it be okay if I use this entrance?"

"It's all straight with me, dude. Not my hotel. You better get another key card, though."

"I'll make sure to do that."

"Good luck with your girlfriend."

"She's not really a girlfriend. Just some girl I met at the bar." Lucas shrugged his shoulders.

"Man, that's even better."

The young man grinned as Lucas passed him to walk through the doorway.

Lucas had visited the hotel's virtual tour the previous week, so he knew the location of Samuel's room. He headed down a small hallway and stopped at the door marked, Stairwell 1. He slipped through the door and climbed floor after floor until he reached his destination. He scanned the ceiling for the surveillance camera, being careful to stay out of its view. Within seconds, he found its location. He timed the camera's loop and dashed for the small housekeeping closet when it was clear to do so. The closet was only a few doors down from where Samuel was supposed to be. He tried the closet door handle. It was unlocked. *More good luck*, he thought as he quickly stepped inside the closet and closed the door. Being careful to avoid making noise, he reached into his coat pocket and removed a yellow envelope. He scribbled a few lines on the coarse paper. For over an hour, he patiently waited in the closet, intent on making sure Samuel was asleep before he approached his room.

When Lucas felt it was safe, he exited the storage closet and positioned himself on the right side of Samuel's room. He peeked at the camera, and timing it just right to stay out of view, he bent down and slid the envelope underneath the door.

When he stood back up, the door next to him was open. A woman in her early forties was standing in the hallway. She cocked her head to the side and stared at him.

*Fucking great.* Lucas winked at the woman and moved closer to her. She smiled at him. He slowly reached into his back pocket and slipped out a small syringe of Propaganician. *Unfortunate for her*, he thought. He noticed a strong odor of alcohol on her. *She's fairly attractive.*

"Hello, are you spying on me?" Lucas displayed a playful grin.

"No. I heard a noise and thought someone was at my door."

"I was just dropping something off for my good friend." Lucas waited for her reaction.

The woman glanced down at her watch. "Hmm, it's midnight. Must be a close friend. You want to be my friend, Mr.

Stranger?" She ran her eyes up and down Lucas' masculine physique. "I love meeting new friends."

Lucas' face became flushed. A tingling sensation pulsed through his male anatomy. *Porn fantasy at the posh hotel.* "I enjoy meeting new people, too," he said in a deep, hushed voice. The camera was moving toward their direction. He knew he had to think of something fast. "Hey, may I join you for a drink?" he asked.

"Hmm, why not?" The woman grabbed Lucas by the arm and pulled him into her room.

When the door finally closed, Lucas sighed with relief.

The woman thrust her tongue in Lucas' mouth, catching him by surprise. He was still holding the thin tube of liquid death in his hand. *Tempting to kill and run.* He reciprocated the sexual advances and undressed her with a hungry passion. It had been months since his last sexual encounter. *Don't do it,* he told himself. The woman forcefully yanked his shirt, causing the buttons to fall off and scatter in several directions. She tugged at his pants and forced her lips upon him. Lucas gripped the syringe in erotic fury and plunged the needle deep into her lower neck. Then he grabbed her head, forced her to the floor, and shoved her face onto the carpet, muffling her attempt to scream. When the Propaganician took effect, he released his grip on her, pulled out the needle, and placed it back into his pocket.

Lucas flipped the woman over. The horror in her eyes made him smile. The combination of discharged bodily fluids and alcohol gave him an idea. Without much care, he lifted the woman onto the bed and removed the rest of her clothing.

It only took him a second to spot the woman's stash of opened wine bottles on the buffet. With much excitement, he walked over, grabbed two of the bottles, and brought them back to the bed. He popped the lid off one of the wine bottles, tilted the woman's head back so that her mouth opened, and emptied the liquid into her waiting orifice. The majority of the alcohol went down her throat. The rest of it spilled onto the silk bedding, creating a red stain around her. He picked up another bottle of wine and took a small sip. *Not bad at all.* He turned the bottle over and emptied the rest of it onto the woman's body. After he was finished, he searched the room for a trash bag. He located one underneath a wastepaper basket. *Perfect!* He placed both wine bottles inside the plastic bag and tied the bag closed.

Lucas searched the room for the woman's personal effects. He found a white handbag, rifled through it, and pulled out the woman's car keys. *Good. I was hoping she didn't valet park.* He returned to the bed and gazed at the shiny band on the woman's wrist. It intrigued him, so he removed it and shoved it into his front pants pocket. *Another trinket to add to my collection.* Lucas hung the do not disturb sign on the outside of the door. *Housekeeping shouldn't bother her for a while.*

With the bag of evidence in hand, Lucas slipped out of the room, being careful to avoid the security camera, and headed to the stairwell. He descended the stairs and entered the indoor parking garage. He grabbed the woman's keys from out of his coat pocket and pushed the red button on the key fob to set off the car alarm. He followed the high-pitched sound. "Ah, there you are," he whispered. He turned off the alarm and walked up to the vehicle. It was a brand new gold Cadillac with lightly tinted windows. He slipped inside, threw the bag of evidence on the passenger seat, and started the engine. The distinct fragrance of peppermint saturated the interior of the car, almost making him gag. He rolled down the windows, preferring to shiver in the cold rather than bear the smell. He drove to the exit and stopped at the parking attendant booth. It was vacant. Lucas let out a sigh of relief.

After driving for several minutes, Lucas spotted the perfect place to leave the car. *This is pretty close to the Honda. Now it will only be a quick jaunt through the woods instead of the long trek I endured getting here.* He parked, rolled up the windows, and shut off the engine. He paused for a moment to reflect on the night's events. *Tonight went differently than expected, but it was quite rewarding.* He had planned on leaving the hotel right after he slipped the note underneath Samuel's door. He didn't plan on indulging in sex and murder. *What a welcome surprise—for me at least. Probably not so welcome for her.* He laughed at the thought that his fortune was her misfortune. His laughter subsided a few seconds later, and he went back to the task at hand. He removed the key from the ignition and threw it under the seat. Then he grabbed the bag of evidence and stepped out of the car. He reached back inside to engage the locks before shutting the door. After one last glance to make sure he didn't forget anything, he sneaked into the darkness and said, "The next time I visit, Samuel will become part of my collection."

# Chapter 23

# Meeting with Kurt

Kelli and Craig were both exhausted when they arrived at Marcona County Hospital. The one-hour drive, mostly through undeveloped land, took a toll on them. The monotonous desert scenery didn't help matters. On top of it all, neither of them had been getting much sleep because of the investigation. Fortunately, when they got out of the car, the frigid outdoor temperatures, along with a gust of cold wind, perked them right up. They walked to the building at a fast pace so they could get out of the cold.

Craig stood next to Kelli while she knocked on Medical Examiner Kurt Delong's office door.

"Come in. It's unlocked," Kurt said.

They entered, and a strong pine oil scent instantly filled their nostrils. The interior was large. A Plexiglass window separated the office from the examination area. Overstocked bookcases lined one side of the room. On the opposite side of the room, Dr. Kurt Delong was sitting at a metallic desk. He seemed oblivious to his guests as he typed on his computer keyboard.

Craig cleared his throat. "Doc, you found something?"

Kurt took off his glasses and rubbed his eyes. "Yes, I was double checking the lab results. Like I said on the message, it appears Propaganician was used again."

"He injected himself?" Craig asked.

"I have to show you." Kurt stood up and walked over to a wall closet. He pulled out two white lab coats and tossed them in their direction. "Put these on."

Kelli hated that part of investigations. She tried to avoid being up close and personal with anyone's internal organs.

"Can't you use your computer to show us?" Kelli pointed in the direction of the desktop.

Kurt cracked a grin. "Not exactly. It won't take long. I promise."

*Great. Just great,* Kelli thought. "As long as it doesn't take too long."

Craig smirked. "Some of us have weak stomachs."

Kelli cast Craig a threatening glare. "Yeah, we do." She slipped into the lab coat.

Kurt opened the door to the exam room and led Kelli and Craig over to a couple of metal tables. Each table had a covered corpse on top of it. Kurt flipped the turquoise sheet off Shauna Holden's body, which had been sliced open from the chest to the groin. Steel clamps held the flesh open, leaving the organs exposed for the world to see. Kelli felt her stomach sink.

Kurt grabbed a medical ruler from a nearby cart and moved closer to the body. "Detectives, I want you to look at the back of her neck. There is a tiny puncture at the base." He placed the edge of the ruler underneath the puncture mark to help them find it. "This is most certainly the location where the Propaganician was injected. I also want you to look at the bruising around her neckline." He moved the ruler around to the various bruises. "These bruises are evidence of massive damage, which tells me that someone powerful forced her head to the floor."

"More powerful than Nesmith over there?" Kelli pointed to the other table.

"Quite a bit more powerful." Kurt pulled the sheet off Grant's body. "Our late Mr. Nesmith is about 140 pounds, which is approximately 10 pounds heavier than the first victim. A blow causing this much damage was created by someone a lot heavier."

Craig bent down and peered at the small hole in Nesmith's skull.

"So, if you're saying what I think, this guy didn't kill Shauna, and he didn't blow his own head off either." Craig shook his head.

"I don't believe he did." Kurt glanced in Kelli's direction and smiled. "Detective Jordan planted a seed in my head when we were investigating the crime scene."

Craig ignored Kurt's last sentence. "Why in the fuck did the gun powder residue test come back positive on him?" Craig asked.

Kurt pointed to Nesmith's right arm. "Look closely at his right index finger. It's bruised. It appears extra pressure caused the bruising."

A thought raced through Kelli's head. "Doc, the real killer physically forced Nesmith to fire the round."

"It makes sense. Let me show you the entry site for the needle on Mr. Nesmith." Kurt picked up a magnifying glass and motioned for both detectives to move closer. "See right there?" Kurt pointed his ruler at the dead man's larynx. "The needle was thrust deeply into this area, and the drug emptied along this area here."

"Seems like the killer knew right where to hit him," Kelli said.

Craig shook his head in disbelief. "If he was murdered, then . . . what . . . somebody made the guy write a suicide note and forced him to confess to killing Shauna Holden? That doesn't make sense."

"Kurt, do you think we are dealing with someone in the medical field?" Kelli asked.

"Too much complexity for it to be anything else," Kurt said. "The wounds on the woman's chest are evidence of that. The location of the injection in the larynx substantiates the theory." Kurt covered both bodies.

"The note and suicide are smokescreens for what?" Craig scratched his head.

"I think we need to look at the security DVD's. Hopefully the footage will show us the guy who did this," Kelli said. She stripped off her gown.

"Be careful, both of you. I don't know how much of this compound your killer has," Kurt warned. "I will check the forensic databases throughout the region for any reports of murders involving Propaganician."

"Good idea. Keep us in the loop," Kelli said. She turned and quickly walked out of the exam room.

"You're welcome. I'll get back to you if I find anything else,"

Kurt yelled out so that Kelli could hear him from the next room.

Kelli waited for Craig in the examiner's office. She thought about what Kurt said and wondered, *Could there be other murders with this drug somewhere else?*

Craig tapped Kelli on the shoulder. "You were right. A killer who uses fake suicide letters and paralyzing drugs sounded a little too out there for me." Craig lifted his hands up in defeat.

"No worries." Kelli smiled.

Who could blame Craig for doubting Kelli? The thought of a man who used drugs to paralyze victims before torturing their bodies was, without a doubt, a lot out there.

Kelli glanced down at her watch and realized it was almost morning. *Pleasure Cove's security footage will be waiting on Craig's desk when we return to the station. The killer tried to fool us. It will prove to be a costly mistake—one he hadn't intended to make,* she thought.

# Chapter 24

# Death Confirmation

---

Lucas arrived home just before dawn. *The woman's car shouldn't be noticed right away*, he told himself. It wasn't a planned kill, so he didn't feel it was appropriate to get too excited about adding her to his collection. *Gotta have a few morals*, he thought. Besides, Samuel was still his main focus. He wished he could be there when Samuel opened the card, but it was just too risky. He hoped the physician would take advantage of his gift. It would make it easier for Lucas.

Murdering Ronald hadn't resolved Lucas' anger. When Ronald killed Brian Jeffers, he took away Lucas' chance of getting back what belonged to him. Lucas still wanted to get it back. He tried to think of a solution. Then something came to him. *What if Ronald was wrong? Maybe he didn't kill Brian Jeffers. I wouldn't put it past the pathetic druggie to make a mistake like that. I have to find out for myself.*

Lucas sat down at his desk and logged on to his laptop. He scanned through the daily headlines of Marcona's local paper. There was no mention of the burnt sport utility vehicle and nothing about Ronald's car being found in the local river.

He navigated to his favorite search engine and typed the words, Desoto Valley Police Chief Brian Jeffers, into the small rectangular box. The results were almost instant. He clicked on the first choice. The Desoto Valley Courier website loaded. Lucas read the article that was on the center of the front page.

## Police Chief and Three Officers Gunned Down

Desoto Valley Police Chief Brian Jeffers (39), Senior Patrol Officer Cordell White (50), Patrol Officer Mike Jansen (40), and Patrol Officer Andrew Pine (27) were gunned down while conducting a traffic stop on 13$^{th}$ Street. The Desoto Valley Police Spokesman identified Ronald Trapp (29) as the suspect. He is also wanted in connection with multiple homicides in four states. There is a manhunt being conducted by local, county, state, and federal law enforcement agencies. If anyone has information on the shooting, contact the Desoto Valley police. A memorial fund at Jackson-Tyson Funeral Home has been established. Viewing of the bodies is private. Graveside service with a police burial will be on Friday at 2 p.m.

Lucas clicked another link, which took him to the Desoto Valley Police Department's website. The police department's website displayed a brief news report about the deaths, along with pictures and short biographies of the murdered officers.

Despite the two news reports, Lucas wasn't convinced that Police Chief Brian Jeffers was dead. He reached behind a stack of folders and pulled out a prepaid cell phone. *Won't be able to trace this.* Lucas had used cash to pay for the phone and the airtime card, and he registered the phone under a fake name and address.

Lucas dialed the phone number that was listed on the police department's website.

"Desoto Valley Police. This is Jennifer speaking," a woman with a harsh sounding voice answered.

Lucas smirked. "Hello, this is Detective Alex Barnum from the Valentine Police Department. I was trying to find some information on Chief Brian Jeffers. He was a good friend of mine."

"Hold one minute, Sir."

Lucas thought about hanging up, but he didn't.

Thirty seconds later, another female voice came on the line and said, "This is Police Information Officer Tricia Stonehouse. How may I help you?"

"Yes, hello. I'm Detective Alex Barnum from the Valentine Police Department. I'm trying to find some information on my former partner."

"Who is that, Sir?" Tricia asked.

"Chief Brian Jeffers."

"Detective, our chief was shot and killed a few days ago. We notified the departments throughout the region."

"I have been on vacation. I'm sorry to hear that. I was just checking to see how the new job was going."

"It's been difficult for us here, Sir. All of these men left behind families. Would you like to talk to Captain Franks? He and Chief Jeffers were friends."

"Sure, maybe there is something I can do for the family." Lucas refrained from laughing.

"I will transfer you to his office. Hold on."

When Lucas heard the line click over, he pushed the end call button. *No more for now.* Tricia Stonehouse didn't sound like she was fucking with him, so he decided to accept the conversation with her as confirmation of Chief Brian Jeffers' demise. *What a pity. Such a pity.* Lucas fingered the heart-shaped jewelry around his neck and exhaled. *This will have to take the place of my cherished coin.*

Brian Jeffers was surfing through the channels on the television when he a heard a knock on his front door. He scrambled to his feet and glanced in the mirror as he rubbed the two-day growth on his face. *Not really ready for company.* He peeked out the curtain and was surprised to see who his visitor was. He smirked as he opened the door.

Tricia Stonehouse had a look of determination on her face as she stepped inside. Brian closed the door and turned her direction.

"Chief, I think we got something," Tricia said. She removed a silver mini voice recorder from her coat.

"Sorry I didn't shave for the occasion." Brian laughed and then grimaced from the pain the laughter caused in his chest. He escorted her to the kitchen and pulled out a chair.

Tricia's lips forced a smile. "The switchboard received a call earlier today. They transferred it to me. I think your plan may have worked."

"What, we actually got a call?" Brian asked.

"We sure did. The guy said he was Detective Alex Barnum

from the Valentine Police Department."

Brian's face tensed up. "He said his name was Alex Barnum?"

"Yes. I did the research on the police database. That was your partner's name, wasn't it, Brian?"

"Actually, he was my supervisor. I found his body. Play the tape, Tricia."

Tricia hit the play button. Brian listened to the complete conversation, knowing the man on the phone was the killer of his former partner.

"I believe this man had Ronald Trapp come after me," Brian said.

"Why not come here himself?" Tricia asked.

"I don't know. What kind of trace did you get?"

Tricia frowned. "I tried to trace, but it was a prepaid phone number." Tricia pulled a green notebook out of her coat pocket and flipped it open. "The number and area code is registered somewhere in North Dakota."

"That's a start. This guy is methodical. He thinks of everything."

"Chief, I think I was convincing enough."

"From the sound of things on the tape, I think you did an excellent job making him believe I was dead," Brian agreed.

"What do you want to do next?" Tricia asked.

"I have something in mind, but for now, let's just keep this information between you and me."

"Are you sure?"

"I'm sure. Right now this asshole thinks I'm dead, and that's exactly what I want him to think."

**Chapter 25**

# Perfect Facade

Kelli Jordan sat at her desk, mindlessly flipping through paperwork. All she could think about was the Pleasure Cove security footage. It had been several hours since the footage was supposed to have been delivered to the police station. Her patience finally ran out. She left her cubicle and headed for Craig's desk to find out what was going on.

Craig was on the phone when Kelli walked into his office. It sounded like he was involved in a heated argument. After a couple of minutes passed, he slammed the handset down onto its base. Then he yanked a pack of cigarettes out of his desk.

"Time for a fucking smoke," Craig said, and then he stormed out of his cubicle.

Kelli followed Craig outside. After they lit their cigarettes, she asked, "What was all that about?"

"Chief Hendricks is talking about involving the feds if we don't come up with something soon."

"How much time is he giving us?"

"We have a week—that's it."

"Not a lot of time to find the bastard." She took a drag from her cigarette. "Hey, I didn't see the strip club DVD."

"Stinson stuck it in the evidence locker downstairs. I'll grab it before we go back up." Craig finished his cigarette and tossed it on the ground. "Stinson said the interim manager had the surveillance tapes stashed behind one of the wall prints in the office."

"At least we got them. Maybe the feds won't need to step all over our investigation." Kelli flicked her cigarette onto a blanket of snow.

"Wishful thinking," Craig said.

Craig swung the door open, and the two of them entered a small office that led to a row of lockers. He removed a small silver key from his pocket and unlocked one of the lockers.

"There it is," Craig said. He pulled a brown paper bag out of the locker and handed it to Kelli.

"It's show time," Kelli said with a big smile on her face. "Let's go take a look and see what we can find on here."

Craig and Kelli took the elevator up to the second-floor conference room and accessed the media review area, which contained several DVD and VCR players. Kelli took the two discs out of the paper bag, threw one on the table, and slipped the other into one of the DVD players. The footage was recorded on a multi-camera, single recorder setup called a switcher security system. The switcher system recorded from one camera at a time, alternating between cameras every few seconds to capture views of different areas of the club. Craig and Kelli stared intently at the video, which was jumping from one part of the club to the next, and tried to spot Shauna.

"I don't see anything with Shauna Holden's performance anywhere," Kelli said with a quizzical look on her face. She fast forwarded the DVD, but there was still no sign of Shauna. Kelli picked up the black DVD case and inspected the date. "This is the one that should have caught Nesmith's killer on camera."

"Wasn't the last one supposed to have Shauna Holden on it?" Craig asked.

"That's what the date on the outside of the case says. Let's see what this other one has for us." Kelli switched DVD's.

"This is looking more fucked up as we go, Kelli." Craig stood up and stared out the window.

The DVD started. The video alternated views showing several different strippers and a few patrons, but there were no sign of Shauna. Kelli was just about to give up when she noticed the date and time on the corner of the screen.

"This is the wrong disc. Look at the date." Shauna pointed at the television screen.

Craig's jaw tightened. "Shit. Someone is playing games with us. The cases don't match the date and time stamps on the surveillance camera."

What the fuck? "The killer knew where the DVD's were, steals them from the scene, and then jacks us around by writing fake dates on the cases!" Kelli ejected the DVD and tossed it on the table.

"I will send Stinson back to the area. Maybe the other discs are there somewhere."

"We're not going to find them. If this psycho had the other DVD's, he has destroyed them by now," Kelli said. She sat down at the conference table, feeling dejected.

"That puts us back at square one," Craig said as he turned off the DVD player.

Kelli brightened up. "We do have something going for us." She tapped the table with her fingernails.

"Please enlighten me," Craig said, sounding as frustrated as he felt.

"The blood left on the money clip. Forensics should have the report done by the end of the day."

"Ah, I wondered when we would get some information back on the blood work." Craig stood up to leave. "I will stop by Chief's office and let him know about the DVD's. He won't be happy."

"I don't think anyone will be happy until we find something that connects us to the killer. I will meet with you later," Kelli said.

Kelli followed Craig out the door. She didn't understand why the killer made such an effort to create a perfect facade. *Maybe the killer is planning something bigger. Maybe this is just the prologue to something even more disturbing.*

# Chapter 26

# A Gift for Samuel

The phone woke Samuel Longnecker out of a deep sleep. He groggily picked up the handset and listened to a computerized voice give him his morning wake-up call. *Busy day for a Saturday*, he thought. His schedule for the day included meetings with several local hospital administrators, lunch with a local media mogul, and a tour of Marcona County Hospital.

Samuel swung his feet off the bed and groaned. He wished he could sleep for another hour, but he didn't have time, so he forced himself to stand up. Something on the ground by the entrance caught his attention. He put his reading glasses on and stumbled over to the mystery object. It was a yellow envelope. He bent down and scooped it up. He opened it and removed two items. The first was a white piece of copy paper. It had a few words in red ink scribbled on the front. The second item was a shiny ticket. Samuel smiled. *Diary of a Peasant is one of my favorite plays. Whoever sent this has incredible taste.* He turned his attention back to the words on the piece of copy paper. Then he turned his head and took a peek at the greeting card on the nightstand. *Is this from the same person? This is strange. Not many people know I am here at this hotel.*

Samuel picked up the phone and dialed the front desk.

"This is Stefan. How may I help you, Sir?"

"Hello, I was wondering if you have any messages for me," Samuel said.

"Mr. Longnecker, let me check your inbox. One moment please." The clerk returned on the line after a few seconds. "I have just one for you, Sir. It's from a Raymond Burrell."

Samuel sighed. Raymond Burrell was Marcona County Hospital's Deputy Director. *He is probably just antsy about meeting later today*, Samuel figured.

"Nothing else?"

"That is the only one, Sir."

"Thanks. I do have one more piece of business while I have you on the phone."

"What may I assist you with, Sir?"

"I'm not driving my car this morning. I need a limousine in about an hour. Can you make that happen for me?"

"I will order it for you, Sir."

"Perfect." Samuel hung up the phone.

Samuel was disappointed that the only message waiting for him was from the hospital employee. The woman he had met at the bar seemed interested in him. *Apparently she was not that interested.* He remembered she said she was staying at the same hotel as him. *Very attractive girl. Might as well give it another shot.* He opened the desk drawer and sorted through the loose change and gas receipts from his trip until he found the folded piece of paper he was looking for. He unfolded the paper and was greeted with the delightful scent of luxurious perfume. He looked at the writing and almost laughed. *She must have been really drunk.* Instead of ink, she used a dark shade of lipstick to write down her information. The smudged makeup was barely legible. It took him a few seconds to make out the words. "Felicity Holt," he said aloud. "Sounds like money." Samuel was a little upset that she left him at the bar after all the dirty talk and flirting she had directed at him, but he was sure spending time with her would make him feel better about it.

Samuel snatched up his cell phone and dialed Felicity's number. After several rings, he hung up. *She must have found another guy. Maybe she checked out.* He picked up the hotel phone and pushed the button for the front desk.

Stefan answered. "Hello, Sir. Was there something else you needed assistance with?"

"Stefan, yes. I'm looking for another one of your hotel guests. It's a business matter."

"Sir, who are you looking for?"

"The name is Felicity Holt. She approached me in regards to a business issue. Has she checked out?"

"Mrs. Holt is still here with us. She is in the Dahlia Suite. That's actually one room down from you. Room 714."

*Figures she's married, but so am I. A cheater for a cheater. Sounds good to me,* Samuel thought. He unconsciously pushed up his glasses. "Really, one room away?"

"Yes. Do you want me to ring her room?"

"I already her cell. She didn't answer. She's probably resting. I will stop by later. Thank you for everything."

"My pleasure. The limousine will be here within the hour for you," Stefan said.

"Thanks! I will see you downstairs." Samuel hung up.

*After my meetings, I will stop by her room,* Samuel told himself. He picked up the letter that he found at the door and looked closely at the red handwriting. Something seemed familiar to him, but he wasn't sure what. He read the words aloud. "The past is not forgotten; it's only hidden from us. Enjoy the play. See ya soon." Samuel remembered someone saying that quote about the past being hidden, but he couldn't remember who he heard say it. *Perhaps my anonymous fan will make him or herself known so that I can offer my thanks in person.*

Samuel glanced at his watch. It was almost time for him to leave. *Maybe when I'm done with everything, it will be time to get with the sultry woman next door. Now that would be a pleasurable experience!* Samuel felt both eager and nervous.

# Chapter 27

# Playing a Hunch

Tricia Stonehouse had been a great help to Brian. She was his eyes and ears to the outside world, and provided him with anything he needed. The reports of his death spread throughout the media, along with other law enforcement agencies, making the charade almost a reality. Misleading the public wasn't what Brian wanted to do, but it was a necessary evil. He was hoping it would bring the killer out in the open.

There were only a handful of people who knew Brian was alive, and that was how he wanted it. His mother-in-law was one of the people who knew. He had to tell her because she was caring for his daughters until the threat of danger was gone.

Brian sorted through several boxes, setting aside three folders in the process. He picked up the folder that contained Ronald Trapp's case files. Most of the files had been prepared by Brian over the years. Brian skipped those and looked at the ones prepared by other officers. He hoped to find something that would help him track down Ronald Trapp.

Ronald Trapp had started his career in crime as a small

town drug dealer in Nebraska. Brian came across Ronald when he had added kidnapping to his forte. The scumbag had enlisted two other smalltime dealers. Together, they decided to grab the mayor's daughter. Brian had just received his promotion to detective and was assigned to the case. Ronald knew Brian was close, so he left his two partners to their own demise. Brian found the girl but was injured during the gun battle. For several months, he had sources looking for Ronald, but nothing ever panned out. Ronald simply vanished. A rash of drug related murders pointed to Ronald Trapp and his thirst to distribute cheap narcotics to the public, but he was never caught.

Brian turned to the last page of the file and was surprised to find that the guy was still married. He jotted down the name of Ronald's wife and picked up the phone to call Tricia.

"Hey, don't you ever sleep?" Tricia asked groggily.

"Now that I'm dead, I probably should," Brian joked.

"If you're calling me this early, you must have found something."

"I was going through Trapp's file and found an interesting little tidbit. He apparently is still married."

"You're fucking kidding?" Tricia suddenly sounded more awake.

"Not at all. Her name is Nina. Write this info down and do a check." Brian recited the details.

"Got it. I will get back to you later. Anything else for me?"

"I'll let you know if I come up with anything else. In the meantime, just work on finding out what you can on Trapp's wife. If you find a criminal file on her, which I'm sure you will, bring it over to me."

"I will give you a buzz if and when I find something," Tricia said.

"Okay. Talk to you soon." Brian ended the call.

Brian picked up the second folder and quickly flipped through it. He set it down and grabbed the last folder. The thought of opening it made him nervous. The folder contained the murder investigation files on his wife and daughter's case. He had never reviewed the contents. The thought of looking at the pictures of their brutalized bodies made him nauseous. Brian grabbed a bottle of vodka and guzzled it down until he had enough courage to view the pictures.

Brian slowly opened the folder. He picked up one picture and analyzed all aspects of the scene. Methodically, he went through each picture. Something odd in one of the pictures caught his eye. The picture was of his living room. The focal point was a trail of blood. There was something much less obvious in the picture that struck Brian as odd. He stared at it. *Leather chair . . . there is something under there.* He brought the picture up to eye level and squinted. *What is that?* He bolted to his office with the picture in hand and snagged a small magnifying glass from an evidence kit. He sat down and positioned the investigative tool over the area of interest. A sudden thought nagged at him. He returned to the living room and grabbed the other pictures. He spread the photos on the floor. All of the pictures had something in common. The carpet looked freshly vacuumed. Sarah wouldn't have missed the item. She always vacuumed under the chairs. *The fifty-cent piece. I found it a few weeks after they were murdered. I didn't think anything of it, until now.*

Brian reached into his evidence kit, pulled out a pair of blue latex gloves, slipped them on, and opened the middle drawer of the desk. He removed the silver coin and gently put it in a plastic bag. *Could this belong to the man who killed my family?* There was one person who could help him find out. Brian picked up the desk phone and dialed a number.

"Forensic Department. Jake speaking."

"Jake, it's Chief. Are you alone?" Brian asked.

"Of course. What can I do you for you?"

"I have something that needs to be analyzed. You got time to stop over and pick it up from me?"

"No problem. What is it?"

"I'd rather not tell you on the phone. It's important though, Jake."

"Okay. Give me like twenty minutes."

"Thanks. Don't tell anyone I called you," Brian directed.

"Lips are sealed, boss. Hey, are you doing all right?"

"Getting there. If this turns out the way I hope, we may have a lead on something bigger. See you when you get here, and thanks for your help." Brian put the receiver back onto the cradle.

Jake was touted as one of the best forensic analysts the state had. With any luck, he could provide some answers. Brian wasn't sure if Ronald Trapp was the sadistic murderer he had been searching for or if someone had planted Ronald in Desoto Valley to carry out another agenda. He had a strong feeling that the answer had something to do with the fifty-cent piece.

# Chapter 28

# Coming Forward

Kelli Jordan took one last drag from her cigarette before she entered the building. The darkened hallways in the police station were ghostly quiet. Craig was supposed to meet her at the forensics office, but he was busy looking into a lead on the part-time morgue employee she had told him about. *On my own for now.* Kelli opened the glass double doors and searched for Andrew Ball.

Andrew Ball was an MIT graduate and one of the lead forensic investigators in the country. Marcona had been lucky to secure his talents. His work on headliner investigations had been paramount in apprehending numerous suspects.

Kelli smiled as she peered at Andrew through a small window. He was faced away from her, working on something that was on the table in front of him. *He is very attractive.* His mid-length, blonde hair and swimmer's build was water cooler gossip with most of the agency's females.

Kelli pulled herself out of her daydreaming and collected her thoughts. She tapped on the window. Andrew turned and motioned for her to enter. She opened the door and stepped inside.

"Detective Jordan, nice to see you. Is your partner going to join us, or are we all alone?" Andrew joked.

"He's busy with something else. It's just us," Kelli flirted back.

"Sorry the results took so long. I had to double-check the original findings."

"What do you mean?" Kelli raised her eyebrows.

"Well, the money clip had two different blood types on the surface." Andrew led her to a table with a microscope. "The victim's and possibly the person who murdered her."

*Now we are getting somewhere.* "Two different types, for sure?" Kelli asked.

"I'm 100 percent certain." Andrew handed her a read-out from the printer. "The first blood type is Shauna Holden's. The second is unidentifiable at this time."

"That's not normal, I take it." Kelli studied the paper.

"Not really. With all the modern day testing, we should have come back with someone." Andrew shrugged.

"Even after running it through national databases, you're still getting nothing?" Kelli tossed the paper onto the table.

"So far, zero results. Doesn't mean we won't find a match," Andrew said with sincerity.

*Fucked again.* "Okay." She sighed. "Honest opinion—what are the chances of finding this guy?"

Andrew looked into the microscope. "I will say fifty percent, if he's in a database anywhere."

Kelli couldn't be upset with him. He was doing his best. "That's better than nothing," Kelli said with resignation.

"I will keep you up to speed if anything comes across the wire." Andrew smiled.

"Keep working on it. I think our killer is going to strike again, and it's going to be soon." Kelli did a quick wave and rushed out the door.

Kelli hurried back to her cubicle and pulled out two cream-colored folders from her drawer. She sat down and studied the crime photos of both Shauna Holden and Grant Nesmith. Her office phone buzzed. It was the front desk weekend police clerk.

"Detective, this is Sally. There is a gentleman up front who says he needs to report something to an investigator." *Shit, something else on my plate.* "Sally, I will be up to talk to him in a moment."

"I will have him wait."

Kelli slammed the phone down, closed the folders, and headed to the reception area.

Right when Kelli entered the police reception area, she noticed the elderly, caucasian man in scraggly clothes. He had a strong pungent odor that suggested he hadn't taken a shower in weeks. He was the only person in the waiting area, so she knew he was the person that had asked for her.

Kelli forced a smile. "Sir, hello. I'm Detective Jordan. How can I assist you?" Kelli started to extend her right hand but thought better of it.

A strong deep voice boomed out of the frail man. "I need to speak at you in your office. You have an office, don't you?"

*Uh oh, sounds like an attitude.* "Of course, follow me," Kelli said in a harsh voice.

"I wasn't going to come down here, but this is important."

Kelli didn't reply. She led the man to her cubicle and

nodded for him to sit in the seat that faced her desk. The man complied. Then Kelli sat down and flipped on her small desk fan, hoping it would blow the man's foul scent away from her. She removed her notebook from the drawer, plopped it on the desktop, and prepared to write.

"Sir, you have something to tell me?"

"Yes, young lady. Name is Martin Bresdine. I live in the old Blacks Window Emporium building. Few nights ago I saw a man kill another." Martin adjusted his seat.

Kelli was a little skeptical. "This was at the Emporium, I take it?"

"Where else would it be, youngster?" Martin asked with contempt.

Kelli shook off the man's rudeness. "Mr. Bresdine, tell me what happened."

The man scooted his chair closer to the desk. "From where I was, I saw the first man stab the other. Then he threw the body in one of those new sport truck things,"

"Did the man drive the truck away?" Kelli asked.

"No, ma'am, he didn't. He put that truck ablaze. Made a marshmallow of that gentleman." Martin chuckled, exposing a toothless smile.

"So, did anyone else see this happen?" Kelli jotted down a few notes.

"No, not that I know of. The building doesn't have a lot of dwellers like me anymore.

*Good for the building.* "Did the fire department come after the car was on fire?" Kelli leaned forward.

"I never saw no one. Fire kept going till the truck went

boom." Martin used his hands to mimic an explosion.

"So the truck is still there?" Kelli really didn't want to ask that question.

"What do you take me for? Of course it's still there," Martin scoffed.

Kelli hesitated. "Could you give me a description of the two men?"

"The man who did the stabbing . . . he was very large. Looked like a muscle man of some kind. The other was sort of scrawny and looked like one of those druggie people."

"Mr. Bresdine, could you identify them if I gave you a few pictures to look at?"

"I could try. Not promising nothing, though."

"Great. That would help us." Kelli wasn't sure whether to believe the man, but he sounded sincere. "Mr. Bresdine, you said the killer set the car on fire?"

"That's right. He blew it up, I'll say."

"Did the other man have a car as well?" Kelli turned on her computer.

"Had one of those sporty types of cars. The maniac man drove off in it."

"You didn't get a look at the license plate, did you?" Kelli logged into the national vehicle database. *Of course not. What am I thinking?*

"I got one of 'em. I wrote the plate down for you all."

Martin reached into his stained coat and removed a store receipt of some kind. "Here ya go. My writing ain't the best, but it was an easy one to remember."

*Wow! He even wrote the state down.* Kelli recorded the

plate in her notes and typed it into the database. About a minute passed before the registered owner's name and picture appeared on the screen. *Ronald Trapp. Where have I heard that name?*

"Do you remember anything else you can tell me?"

"I don't think there's too much left to tell. One man killed another. Now he's out there. He might even kill me."

"I will have someone bring pictures down for you to look at. Give me a moment, please."

Kelli ran a search on Ronald Trapp's name in the criminal database. The screen immediately filled with a warning to law enforcement officers nationwide. Kelli's eyes widened as she read the information. Ronald Trapp was wanted for drugs, arson, kidnapping, and for the recent murder of four law enforcement officers in Colorado. *Why would he come here?* Kelli looked up at the displaced man and smiled.

"You have been a great help. I'm going to call my partner, and we're going to check out this information. Thanks. Really! I'm going to get somebody over here now to show you some pictures."

Kelli made a quick phone call to the evidence department.

Within a few minutes, a plainclothes officer arrived. After a brief introduction, he escorted Mr. Bresdine to the evidence viewing room.

After they left, Kelli picked up the phone and called Craig.

Craig answered after the first ring. "What's up, Kelli?"

"Maybe something. I'm not sure. You know where the old Blacks Window Emporium building is?"

"Yeah, in the middle of fucking nowhere. Did something

happen there?

"Meet me there in thirty minutes. Might be a dead body over there."

"Fuck! That doesn't surprise me. Lots of homeless in that area."

"Not a homeless person. A real-time dirt bag could be our victim," Kelli said.

"Well, that changes everything. Okay, I'll meet you in a bit."

"Hey, did you find anything out about the part-time morgue guy?" Kelli asked while crossing her fingers.

"Nope. Big, fat, greasy donut. What about the blood work on that money clip?"

"Two types of blood. One is obviously Shauna Holden's. The other . . . Andrew couldn't tell for sure. He's looking through all available databases for a match." Kelli realized she slipped by using the forensics expert's first name.

"Andrew, hmm, sounds like you're joining the water cooler whores," Craig teased.

"Okay, asshole. You can fuck off now. Thirty minutes—at the Emporium. See you then." Kelli hung up.

Kelli grabbed her coat and exited through the rear of the building. She was sort of disappointed the information on the morgue attendant didn't come to something more solid, but she realized that if Ronald Trapp was dead in a burnt out vehicle, something bigger was going on in Marcona.

# Chapter 29

# Burnt Discovery

 Kelli carefully turned onto the slippery gravel, being mindful of the snow packed ditches. *Don't need to have an accident now.* The condemned structure, formally known as Blacks Window Emporium, was almost invisible in the blizzard-like conditions. She pulled her car in front of the building. From what she could see, nobody was around, but the snow severely limited her view. She looked down at her cell phone. The small bars, which usually showed a strong signal, indicated that she had no reception at all. "Shit. Figures this would happen," Kelli muttered. She flipped a button on the police radio and pressed the push to talk button.

"30-58 to Dispatch," Kelli said.

"Dispatch. Go ahead," a woman responded.

"I'm at the old Blacks Window Emporium building. My cell is down out here. Send me a back-up unit."

"10-4. I will have a patrol unit available in the next ten minutes. You okay out there?" the dispatcher asked.

"10-4, Dispatch. 30-53 will be joining me in a few." The radio squelched a little as Kelli released the talk button.

"Roger that. I will advise the patrol unit."

"Thanks. I will be out on the portable."

Kelli clipped the handset back onto the metal holder. She opened the glove compartment and removed a hand-held police radio. She turned it on, stepped outside, and clipped it to her belt.

Kelli looked at the condemned structure in front of her. She was impressed by the size of the once prosperous Blacks Window Emporium building. Many of the large windows were broken out. The faint glow of candles or small lighting devices of some kind were scattered throughout the structure. *People actually try to live here?*

Kelli walked to the far corner of the building and spotted a long driveway that ran along the entire back of the structure. The entrance of the driveway was blocked by a few feet of snow. *The car can't get over or around that. Just wonderful.* She climbed over the snow bank and made her way up the icy road.

Shiny pieces of metal were scattered in various directions along the ground, over an area of several hundred feet. *Could this be the car that Martin Bresdine was talking about?* Kelli wondered. She continued walking through the knee-high mounds of white snow. She passed by a bumper and something that looked like a muffler. The wind and snow were pummeling her face with fury, but she kept moving forward. She squinted to better see ahead of her and spotted the frame of a sport utility vehicle. It was partially covered with snow, but it fit the description the homeless man had provided. She inched her way closer, being careful not to contaminate a possible crime scene. Her portable radio came to life.

"30-58 from 30-53, what's your location?" Craig Berte's voice blasted from the small speaker.

"Behind the main building. Follow the road for two hundred feet. It curves a little and continues for another couple hundred feet. I've got something here—I think."

"10-4. Is there another way around without going through the snow?" Craig asked.

"Negative. That's the only way." Kelli chuckled at how lazy her partner could be.

"10-4. A patrol unit should be with us soon."

"Okay. I'm checking this thing out. Looks like a burned vehicle, just like our guy said." Kelli moved closer to the vehicle frame.

"10-4. I should be there soon." Craig sounded a little out of breath.

Kelli reached the vehicle. She brushed away the snow to get a better look at what was inside. The windows were blown out and the exterior metal was heavily charred. The recent snow had blanketed the interior, so she couldn't tell if there was something underneath. She reached into her coat pocket, pulled out a pair of latex gloves, slid them on, and forced the vehicle door open.

Using just her hands, Kelli began clearing the snow off the vehicle frame. After a few minutes of clearing off the snow, she suddenly jumped back and cried out, "Shit!." A human skull, scorched beyond all recognition, was staring up at her. A pulpy substance replaced where the eyes had been. The mouth was stuck in a frozen state of horror. Kelli became queasy and had to look away for a moment so she wouldn't vomit on the crime scene.

Kelli hit the transmit button on the radio. "30-58 to 30-53, where the fuck are you at?"

"About one hundred yards from you. What's wrong?"

"I found some remains in the truck. Radio the identification unit and medical examiner."

"10-4. I will also call for a city plow to come clear the area," Craig said.

"Good idea. Looks like it's going to be a long one."

"10-4."

Kelli rushed to the front of the sport utility vehicle and stopped next to what remained of the driver's side window. She pulled the latex gloves off her hands. Her fingers were close to frostbitten. She leaned forward, being careful to avoid the remaining bits of glass, and pushed the snow away from the lower side of the front dashboard to uncover the vehicle identification number. The numbers were partially covered by melted plastic. She pulled a small tactical knife out of her front coat pocket and tried to scrape the plastic away. She was so engrossed with the task that she didn't hear Craig approaching. He scared the crap out of her when he trampled up next to her.

"Fuck," Kelli shouted.

"Startled you, huh?" Craig laughed.

Kelli pushed Craig's shoulder and started laughing as well.

"There are pieces of this thing everywhere," Craig said. "I found one of the license plates for you." He extended his gloved hand to show her the find.

"That's a start. The VIN number is almost fucking melted off. I have most of it, though." Kelli tapped her knife against the dashboard.

"The snowplow is on the way. So is your medical examiner boyfriend," Craig teased.

Kelli gave him a warped smile and extended her middle finger to address his inappropriateness.

"Here's a question for you, Kelli. Somebody burns this bastard. For what reason?

When we find the owner of this truck, maybe he will tell us."

Craig held out the license plate again.

Kelli pointed to the letters on the license plate. "That plate doesn't belong to this truck."

"Huh. What the fuck are you talking about?" Craig cocked his head.

"It belongs to a dark sedan. Ronald Trapp owns a dark sedan."

"So the guy who fried him, changed the plates?" Craig walked back to the rear of the truck.

"Spot-on, Sherlock," Kelli teased as she followed Craig.

"That makes little to no sense." Craig peered through the busted window.

"I'm not surprised. Has anything made sense in the past five days?" Kelli avoided looking at the gruesome sight.

"Point taken." Craig motioned toward the skeleton and asked, "So where is this guy's car?"

"My guess is that it was abandoned." Kelli scanned the area for other vehicles. She didn't see any.

"Abandoned with the plates belonging to this car on it?

"Exactly." Kelli pointed at him.

"Just wonderful." Craig slapped the truck with his hand.

"You want to know something else?" Kelli asked.

"Not really. This is more than enough." Craig looked away.

"The person who owns this truck is probably dead." Kelli raised her eyebrows.

"Where did you come up with that?" Craig asked with a disgusted look on his face.

Kelli tapped the top of her head and said, "The same way I knew Nesmith's suicide and confession were fake. "

Craig shrugged. "Okay, I'll give you one for the suicide, but this new theory is even a bigger stretch."

They heard sirens approaching and ended their discussion.

Kelli tried to make sense of everything. *If the skeletal remains are Ronald Trapp's, then he had to have shown up here for a reason. The man killed four police officers in another state. Now he shows up dead. It seems like someone went to great lengths to get him to come here. I need to find out why.*

# Chapter 30

# An Unexpected Call

Lucas opened the daily paper and was ecstatic about the clip he found. *Too bad I couldn't keep a memento, but I can add this clipping to my wall of fame.* He cut out the short article about Grant Nesmith and hung it up. Then he stepped back and stared at it, cherishing the memory of Grant's murder and feeling proud of his own ingenuity. *By the time the police figure out how Nesmith really died, I will be long gone.*

Lucas peeked down at his watch. *I wonder if Ronny has been found.* He turned on the television. It was already set on the local news channel. All that showed on the screen was static. Lucas gave the ancient device a tap on the side. The picture improved but was still blurry. The sound was fine. Lucas turned up the volume. He heard the local weatherman talking. *I must have missed the news.*

Lucas walked over to his workbench and pulled his new project out from underneath it. The oversized container was heavy. He had to use both hands to lift it to the top of the table. He yanked off the white cover and checked it for damage. It was in good order. He opened the row of cabinets adjacent to the table and removed several filled jars. He unscrewed the first, releasing a putrid odor that almost knocked him off his feet. He dumped the murky liquid into the container. He repeated the process with each jar. *Should be the perfect amount,* Lucas' thought. The local news anchorman's voice caught his attention. He went over to the TV and listened.

"This is Brock Fetters reporting with a breaking news story. An anonymous tip led Marcona City Police to an abandoned business on the east side of the county. A man's remains were found inside a burned vehicle at the scene. Police Spokesman Robert Meeks stated that the department suspects the man burned to death while sleeping in his vehicle. For unknown reasons, possibly due to a gas leak, the vehicle exploded, sending debris several hundred feet in all directions. At this time, the identity of the victim is unknown. The county medical examiner is on the scene, investigating the matter. We will keep you posted as details become available."

Lucas smiled. *Nothing linking me there. The aquarium will be ready in a few days. Just in time for Samuel.* Lucas picked up his label maker and typed in the name of his most prized conquest. He eased open the cabinet and was just about to attach the plastic label onto one of the drawers when his prepaid cell phone rang. A strange look came over his face as he reached for it.

"Hello, this is Patrick," he said with uncertainty in his voice.

"Is this my husband's friend? a woman asked.

"How did you get this number?" Lucas grabbed a pen to write down the woman's phone number from the caller ID.

"I'm looking for my husband . . . my husband, Ronald. The

bastard gave me this number in case I needed to speak with him," the woman said.

*Ronald will be responsible for his wife's death.* "Ronald is out. Should be back later. He didn't tell me he had given my number out."

"He said to call if I hadn't heard from him in a few days. It's been a few days."

*Probably worried Ronald is cheating on her.* Lucas laughed. "That's sweet of you to call. Like I said, Ronald stepped out. He's running a small errand for me."

"What kind of errand are you having him do for you?" the woman asked and scolded him at the same time.

"Just a little business—that's all."

"That fucker needs to stay out of trouble. The police people stopped by the house today. You know why?"

"No, I can't imagine what they would want with him," Lucas lied.

"This detective said my Ronny killed a few police officers."

"I can assure you, you're husband has been with me for the last few days. He hasn't been out of my sight." Lucas smiled.

"Who are you anyway?" the woman asked.

"Call me Patrick. What's your name?"

"I'm Nina," she said, relaxing her tone.

"Well, Nina, your husband is busy doing something very important for me."

"Patrick, I'm losing the signal on my phone."

"Where are you at?"

"I ditched the cops. They were following me at the mall. I stole a car, and now I'm driving west on I-80. I'm headed up there to see my Ronny."

*Never a shortage of dumb people to kill.* "Did he give you an address to meet him at?" A worried look spread across Lucas' face.

"Patrick, I'm about to lose you. We planned on meeting tomorrow in Blythe. There is a huge truck stop there."

Lucas knew right where it was. "I will let Ronald know."

"Patrick, the police said they were looking for his sedan."

*I'm sure they are,* Lucas thought. "Nina, we will ditch it. My car is a silver Honda. Look for it at the truck stop."

"Thanks for your help, Patrick. I will try to give you a call before I get close."

"Nina, they will be monitoring your phone. Get rid of it and pick up a prepaid one." The line went dead. Lucas hung up and looked at his phone. *Have to get rid of this one as well.*

Lucas needed to alter his schedule to make room for another unexpected death. He wasn't fond of unplanned murders. They were risky. He especially didn't want to get caught when his perfect masterpiece was just around the corner. After thinking about the situation for a moment, he realized he didn't need to worry. *Nothing will get in my way. Nina obviously is as dumb as Ronald was. I can handle her easily.* Excitement pulsed through his veins. He massaged the heart-shaped necklace and fantasized about his upcoming rendezvous with Samuel.

# Chapter 31

# Truth Exposed

Brian Jeffers showed Jake all the pictures from the crime scene and told him the theory he had come up with. Jake didn't seem to think the story was too far-fetched. Brian instructed the researcher not to advertise their private meeting. He trusted that he would keep his secret.

Jake led Brian through a series of hallways and stopped in front of a darkened office. He took a plastic card out of his pocket and inserted it through a slot above the cipher lock. A green light above the door flashed, and the door slowly opened.

Brian chuckled. "Now I know where all the money goes."

Jake smiled and whispered, "A little perk here and there makes Jake a happy boy." He eased the door open and hit the wall switch. The fluorescent lights blinked for a few seconds before becoming fully functional.

Brian shielded his eyes. "Sort of like a mad scientist's lair," he quipped.

"You're just jealous." Jake escorted Brian through another interior room. "Make yourself at home. I'm going to fire up the machines."

"Great. Thanks for doing this." Brian sat down in a large cushioned chair.

"That's what I do. Besides, if you're right about that coin, maybe we can find out a thing or two."

Jake walked out of the room. He returned a few minutes later in a lab coat.

"I was right about the mad scientist thing." Brian laughed, causing pain in his chest. He grabbed at it and took a few deep breaths.

"I told you in the car, I don't think it is cool for you to push yourself this hard," Jake scolded him.

"I will be all right . . . keep forgetting that I'm still healing," Brian said as he tapped his chest and smiled.

"Okay, enough said on my part then, let's check out this coin." Jake removed the transparent evidence bag from another larger bag. "Follow me."

Brian slowly got to his feet and followed the analyst through the metallic door. The interior work area looked like it belonged to NASA. There were rows of computers lining both sides of the walls, and two shiny titanium tables in the center of the room. One table was filled with equipment, ranging from beakers to several odd devices that Brian couldn't identify. The equipment that impressed him the most were the two large screen monitors affixed to the wall.

Brian gave Jake a suspicious look and said, "I guess you are the right guy."

"I told you there are a few perks."

Jake removed the coin from the evidence bag and placed it on a rectangular, metal plate. He grabbed a small bag of swabs, removed one, and ran the cotton tip along the edges of the coin. Then he placed the swab in an open sterilized tin. He repeated the process with several more swabs. When he was done, he reached over and removed a clear bottle of liquid from a wooden box. He poured some of its contents on the first swab. The white cotton tip instantly turned a shade of red. Jake shook his head and looked up at Brian.

"What's up?" Brian leaned over to observe him.

Jake picked up the swab with a gloved hand. "This is blood. The coin you have been carrying has remnants of human blood on it."

"Blood?" Brian was excited, which caused his chest to throb.

"Yes, it's blood. I'm going to check all these swabs. There may be more than one type involved." He held the tinted swab up for Brian to see.

"Can you find out whose blood it is?" Brian asked.

"Once I'm done processing the samples, I will run them through our national database for a match." Jake was already pouring the liquid on the remaining swabs.

"This is the killer's. I know it."

"Brian, wait a sec. We don't know whose this is. Let me do the testing, okay?"

Brian didn't want to be impatient, especially since Jake had been so helpful. "Okay, I know it's crazy to jump the gun, but Jake, my radar tells me something else."

"It's amazing that there's still any evidence on the coin. Wherever you had it stored may have preserved it, which of course leads me to my next question.

Brian knew where Jake was going with his inquiry so he answered before he was even asked. "It's just been sitting in my desk, and sometimes in my pocket."

"No shit?" Jake responded as he watched the remaining swabs turn the same color.

"Yeah, I can't believe it took this long for me to figure it out."

"Can't worry about that now, Brian. The mind gets all fucked up when something traumatic happens. Come look at the other swabs."

"More blood?"

"On every single swab," Jake said.

Brian's pulse quickened. "When do you think we will know something?"

"It will take a few days." Jake placed the swabs into a small freezer unit. "I will get the results to you as soon as possible."

"Like I said earlier, let's keep this on the down low," Brian reminded Jake.

"Not a word. You can count on it."

Jake escorted Brian to his car.

All Brian could think about during the drive back to his house was the blood on the fifty-cent piece. *I almost got you now.* The noose around the killer of his family was being placed into position.

# Chapter 32

# Materializing Lead

 Dusk had fallen on the crime scene by Blacks Window Emporium. The frozen temperatures had made it too difficult to collect evidence. Detectives Kelli Jordan and Craig Berte tried to interview the homeless people strewn throughout the building, but it was slow going. Most of them were very reluctant to become involved.

Kelli peered down at her watch. *Ten hours. Time for a smoke.*

Craig saw Kelli turn to leave the area. He went up to two officers that had been standing nearby and said, "We haven't had any luck getting any of the homeless people to talk. Go see what you can get out of them?" Without waiting for a response, Craig walked away and headed the direction that Kelli had gone.

Craig caught up with Kelli just as she reached the exit door and said, "Not a fucking one of them saw anything. Can you believe that?"

"Does it surprise you?" Kelli opened the door that led outside.

"I guess it doesn't. I sent two other uniformed officers to

interview the homeless. Maybe they can get some info."

"Well, I hope you wished them luck. They will need it." Kelli took a cigarette from the almost empty pack. "Shit, I'm almost out of smokes. What else can go wrong?" She turned away from the wind to light her cigarette.

"The medical examiner is still out there. I wonder if he has found anything." Craig puffed on his own cigarette.

"More than us, I suppose," Kelli said.

Craig shrugged. "Probably true. Let's go find out. It's too fucking cold to stand here."

"You got that right." Kelli took a few more hits from her cigarette before flicking the butt onto the snow. "Okay, let's go."

The path to the burnt vehicle had finally been cleared, which made it a relatively quick walk. Craig and Kelli stopped at the rear of the medical examiner's van. Kelli knocked. Kurt opened the door and smiled.

"How is the canvassing for witnesses coming?" Kurt asked.

"For shit. How's it going in here?" Kelli crooked her neck and peeked inside.

"About the same as you. I will be leaving for the county morgue in a few." Kurt zipped up the black body bag and covered it with a blanket. "If you want to come along, you're welcome to."

"I'll pass for now. Still have to meet with the fire investigator. Maybe he can give us some info on what was used to start this inferno."

"I will be checking the deceased's dental records. It should take a day or so to get confirmation back," Kurt said.

"No worries," Craig said. "Kelli thinks it's some guy named Ronald Trapp."

Kurt rubbed the stubble on his chin. "Well, sounds like we have a starting point." He looked at Kelli and asked, "You are feeling a vibe on this?"

Craig shook his head in disgust and turned to leave. As he was walking away, he called out to Kelli, "I gotta check on something, partner."

Kelli ignored Craig. "Yeah, this fucking thing isn't sitting right with me," she said.

Kurt was interested. "What are you thinking?"

"This vehicle had the plates from Trapp's car. My instinct is telling me that the burned remains are Trapp."

"Hmm, when you get done here, head to your office and see if this Trapp guy has a prison record. If he does, find out which one he went to. I can make a phone call and get the dental records faxed over," Kurt said. He gave her a look of confidence.

Kelli was glad someone believed her. "Thanks. It means a lot."

"We all have our hunches. I hope this is right for both of us. I will talk to you later. Gotta get our victim to the lab."

"Sure. I will find out that information and keep you posted," Kelli said."

Kurt shut the van door and drove away. Kelli trudged through the snow and met with Craig.

"Kurt going to his office?" Craig asked.

"Back to the morgue to work on the victim."

"I'll wait here for the fire dude. Go ahead and get some

chow. I'll meet you at the office later." Craig waved her off.

"Good idea," Kelli said. "I need to look up a few things, anyway."

Kelli retreated to her car. She got to thinking about the three cases. *The killer, or killers, seemed to plan almost a perfect setting for each murder. Most murders are predictable, but not these.* She put the car in gear and took off toward the police station.

Kelli sat down at her desk and turned on the laptop. She typed in her password. Notification of the newly installed system popped up on the screen.

The Police Information Network, or PIN as the tech guys called it, was supposed to be the best money could buy. The chief of police was a strong supporter of the technology, seeing it as a valuable opportunity to align his department's system with the larger departments.

After the notification window closed, Kelli clicked on the vehicle information search icon. A screen opened, requesting automobile demographics. She pulled out her notebook and flipped to the page that contained the partial VIN she had gotten from the burned vehicle. She copied the partial VIN into the search screen. After several minutes, the PIN system came back with a list of over 2,500 possibilities.

*Shit.* Kelli realized the search was going to take a bit of time, so she took a break to stop at a late night deli and pick up a turkey club and drink.

When Kelli arrived back at the station, she had a full stomach and was ready to get back to work. She sat at her desk and grabbed a pair of dark-rimmed glasses from her middle drawer. *What a sight*, she thought. Kelli had been issued the glasses while in the military, and had continued to use them since. She put the glasses on to temper the harsh florescent lighting. *Much better*, she thought.

Kelli printed the list of VIN's, figuring paper would be easier on her eyes than a small computer screen. She flipped through the pages and studied the information. A few hours later, just as she was about to take a break, she found a match. She highlighted the VIN with a yellow marker. Her pulse quickened. *This is it. Right type of vehicle and the numbers match.* She entered the VIN in the system. A picture of Marissa Hodges popped up on the screen. The woman was thirty-nine years old, had jet-black hair, and an olive complexion. The data on the screen also showed that the woman had a second vehicle registered in the county.

Kelli snatched the glasses off her face and rubbed her eyes. She looked down at her watch. It was almost midnight. *I hope this woman is alive.* She picked up the desk phone handset and dialed Craig's cell phone.

"Craig here."

"Hey, Craig. I got a lead on the owner of the truck."

Craig was talking to someone else at the same time Kelli was talking to him, but he heard what she said, and he was eager to share his news with her as well. "I got something, too. Just got done talking to William Kelly. He's the fire investigator assigned to this case. He says the back interior of the truck had been drenched with lighter fluid."

Kelli penned down a few notes on her yellow notepad. "Hey, did you hear what I said? Kelli snapped at him. She was tired, and it was taking a toll on her patience. "The Tahoe belongs to a woman named Marissa Hodges. She lives at 1217 Ravenwood Drive. It's on the east side of the city."

"I'm almost finished up here, finally. Where does she live again?" Craig asked.

"1217 Ravenwood Drive, on the east side. Why don't you grab a patrol unit and meet me over there," Kelli said as she printed up a photo of the woman.

"10-4. How did you find her?"

"The new PIN system. It fucking actually works. Had to sort through a shit load of pages to find the VIN, but I got it." Kelli grabbed the photo off the printer and put it with her other files in her bag.

"Well, sounds like it works. I'll call a unit and meet you over at the woman's house." Craig hung up.

Kelli rushed out the door and headed straight to her car. She pulled the portable red light out from under her seat, set it up on the dashboard, and plugged the adapter into the lighter outlet. *It's late. Gotta hurry.* She turned the portable light on and sped out of the lot, hoping Marissa Hodges was either out of town or using the other car she had registered, but her gut feeling told her something evil was waiting to be discovered.

# Chapter 33

# Finding Marissa

Kelli Jordan turned the red flashing light off and slowly pulled up in front of Marissa Hodges' house. The driveway and sidewalk were packed with snow. Garbage was overflowing the confines of the trash cans. The brown stucco residence was surrounded with pine trees, making it near impossible to see what was inside. Kelli picked up the radio handset and pushed the button on the side.

"30-58 to Dispatch," Kelli said.

A young, deep, male voice responded. "Dispatch. Go ahead with your traffic."

"Advise the patrol unit to deactivate emergency lights upon arrival," Kelli ordered as she grabbed another full magazine clip from the armrest storage compartment.

"10-4, 30-58. We're dialing the home now to see if we can make contact with the owner," the dispatcher said.

"10-4. I'm waiting for 30-53 before approaching the house."

"10-4. We dialed the number. Unable to make contact with anyone inside. You copy, 30-58?"

"10-4. Thanks for trying." Kelli eased the driver's side door ajar.

"30-58, also be advised two patrol units are en route to your location. Do you want them to set up in a special area?"

"10-4. There is an alley opposite the residence. Have one of the patrol officers respond from that way. Have him switch to channel three when he arrives," Kelli commanded.

"Will advise the unit."

Kelli looked in the rearview mirror and noticed Craig was coming down the street. He turned off the red and blue light bar as he stopped twenty feet behind her. She snatched her portable radio from the glove compartment and exited the car. Craig met her halfway.

"Hey, anything so far?" Craig asked. He nodded in the direction of the residence.

"Nothing yet. Dispatch tried to call. No answer, though."

"What's the plan?"

"We don't know what we have. Let's play it close to the vest. If the woman is dead, someone might be using this as a place to stay.

"Are you serious? Craig shook his head.

"I'm serious. Here's what we got going. One patrol unit is coming in from the alley behind the house. We will use the pine trees as cover."

"Shit, the whole fucking house is covered with trees. Do you think anyone could shoot through them? I can barely see through 'em."

"You want to take that chance?" Kelli folded her arms across her chest.

"Course not." Craig held up his hands in defeat.

The other patrol unit arrived and parked one house away from where the detectives were. Kelli motioned for the officer to remain by the garage. She lifted her jacket and withdrew her nickel-plated 9mm semi-automatic. Craig held up three fingers, which was the signal to turn the portable radio to channel three for localized communication. Kelli repeated the signal to the other officer.

Craig sprinted to one side of the house; Kelli went to the other. Kelli prayed nothing would go bad, but she mentally prepared herself in case it did. They both looked around to see if the coast was clear. Seeing that it was, Kelli plodded though the snow, moving quickly to the side of the front door. Craig peeked through a pine tree on the opposite side, with his weapon in a position to cover her. Kelli extended her arm and grasped the handle of the screen door. It creaked as she opened it. Craig moved a little closer to get a better view of the door.

When Kelli reached out to knock on the door, she noticed it was already partly ajar. She motioned for Craig to come closer as she pushed on the wooden surface. *No fucking noise inside at all.* Her heart sped up. Even though it was below freezing, small beads of perspiration started to form on her brow. She removed the tactical flashlight from her belt and clipped it to the attachment below her weapon's muzzle. Then she pushed the door all the way open.

"Marcona Police, anybody in here?" Kelli shouted.

The eerie sound of silence greeted Kelli. She forced herself to step through the doorway.

"Marcona Police. We are armed. Is anyone here?" Kelli shouted even louder than she had the first time.

Kelli moved into the interior room, training the powerful beam of the flashlight in front of her. She didn't notice it at first, but the house was way too cold. She aimed the flashlight up and down the walls as she searched for a light switch. *There we are.* She moved to the wall and flipped the switch. *No luck.* She passed in front of an air duct and noticed cold air was blasting out from it. *The house has power.* She looked up. *No bulb in the light fixture.* She saw Craig step up to the doorway.

Kelli tapped the microphone on her radio and said, "All units on channel three, keep your eyes open. I'm moving to the hallway. Nothing here so far."

"10-4. You feel that cold air?" Craig asked.

"The central air is on. It's a little strange." Kelli replied as she moved cautiously through the narrow corridor.

"You bet it's strange," Craig said. He scanned the room, looking for another source of light.

Kelli crept along the wall. She observed three doors on the opposite side of the hallway. She reached out and cracked open the first. *Nothing here either.* The room appeared to be a storage area. It was filled with a few pieces of exercise equipment, along with several cardboard boxes.

Craig took up a position behind Kelli. He watched for unseen threats as she postured in front of the next door. Kelli grasped the knob and turned it. The door wouldn't budge. *What the fuck.* She motioned for Craig to give her a hand. He forced his weight against the door. It still didn't move.

Kelli pushed the button on her radio and said, "30-58 to

patrol unit."

"Go ahead 30-58," the patrol officer responded.

"Check on the north side of the house for a window. Advise me on what you find," Kelli said.

"10-4, Detective."

Both Craig and Kelli pushed against the door, using much more force than before, but still, no luck. Craig tried kicking the wooden barrier, but only a few pieces of chipped paint dropped to the ground.

"What is blocking it?" Craig backed away.

"We're about to find out," Kelli said.

Kelli walked up to the last room, opened the door and stepped inside. Craig followed her. Kelli reached for the wall switch and flicked it on. A light came on, filling the room with a soft red glow. Kelli looked up. The light was coming from two lamps, one on each side of the room. *This is the master bedroom*, she determined.

Craig crept next to a long oak dresser. Several framed photographs stretched along the surface.

"Is this the woman who owns the Tahoe?" Craig asked. He picked up a wedding picture and showed it to Kelli.

Kelli glanced at the picture. "That's her. Now all we have to do is find out where she is."

"Is that all?" Craig asked sarcastically. He returned the photo to the dresser.

"Patrol unit to 30-58," the officer said over the portable radio. "The window is open. Oh crap, what the fuck," the patrol officer's voice cracked, "there's a body hanging on the back of the door."

"Repeat your traffic," Kelli said.

"There's a body . . . ripped open . . . hanging from the door," the patrol officer said.

Kelli turned to Craig. "I fucking knew it. I'll call dispatch and get the identification team on the way." She switched the radio channel back to its original settings.

"30-58 to Dispatch."

"Dispatch. What's your status?"

"Dispatch, we need an identification team at this address, along with a county coroner. You copy?"

"10-4. I will send them to your location," the dispatcher said.

Kelli bolted up the hallway and through the front door. She crashed through tree branches, causing minor injury to her face and neck. She forced herself to continue moving forward, and a few seconds later, found herself standing next to the patrol officer who had relayed his gruesome discovery. The newly trained officer appeared fixated on a sight so horrific that he wouldn't have a peaceful night sleep for the rest of his life. Kelli looked through the window, instantly recognizing the woman from the photo in the police database. *Oh fuck!*

Marissa Hodges was naked, spread eagle on the backside of the door. The back of her head was embedded on the hanging door hook, forcing her eye sockets to pop out and hang aimlessly, only connected by the nerves. There was a Y incision gouged in the center of her torso. Layers of skin had been filleted away to create a gaping hole. The internal organs had been removed. Only a hollow shell remained. When Kelli poked her head closer, she saw why the two of them couldn't open the door. A very large air conditioning unit was propped against the wooden entryway. It was on, shooting blasts of cold air from the vents.

That bastard was trying to keep the area cool so that we couldn't figure out the time of death. Kelli raised her fists and pummeled the stucco siding repeatedly, using all the force she could muster, until she slumped to the ground out of complete exhaustion.

# Chapter 34

# Nina's Nightmare

Lucas smiled when he spotted the perfect place to park his beat up Honda. The mall wouldn't be open for a few more hours. Several of the food court workers had already arrived, early as usual, to prep the ingredients for the day. The workers that had not yet gone inside, stayed to themselves and didn't even give Lucas a second look. Lucas popped the trunk and removed a brown, leather case. Then he closed the trunk and walked away from the car with the leather case in his hand. He buttoned up his black trench coat as he quickened his pace across the parking lot. After a couple of minutes, he reached a small wall that divided the mega mall from his other destination. He climbed over the wall and landed in front of a building.

Lucas brushed himself off before entering the building. A young woman in her early twenties was behind the counter, engaged in a telephone conversation. Lucas flashed a smile at her. She returned the gesture. *Very appealing and even sexy,* Lucas thought. He found himself staring at the woman's tight blue sweater and, most of all, her voluptuous curves.

The woman hung up the phone, turned her attention to

Lucas, and said, "Hello, my name is Allison. Welcome to Stark Rental. How may I assist you today?"

"Hi, Allison, I'm Patrick. I need a car. Just for today."

"Very good. I'm glad you decided to use us for your travel needs," Allison said in the cliché format her employer would be most proud of.

"I was looking at the silver Honda out there." Lucas pointed to the rental car parking lot.

Allison smiled. "Let me check and make sure we don't have it on reserve for someone." She tapped on the keyboard. "You're in luck. It's got a full tank and is ready for travel."

"Great. I just need it for the day. Won't be later than 10:00 p.m." Lucas glanced down at his watch.

"No problem, Sir. The charge for the day is the same as for the overnight," Allison said.

"Regardless, I promise to have it back at 10:00 p.m." Lucas mentally calculated how long it would take to rid himself of Nina Trapp. "Possibly a slight bit later, but definitely before morning."

Allison explained the rental contract details. Soon after, she handed Lucas the keys to the Honda. He got in the car and headed to meet Nina Trapp.

Nina Trapp gawked at the exit sign. She was anxious to see Ronny. To her, the thought of him killing four police officers in Colorado was crazy. Ronny was a small-time drug dealer who had little aspiration of becoming anything better. She had met him when she was just a college freshman, and he was selling cocaine throughout the dorms. Nina wasn't stupid by any means, but her radar for finding good men had been in a state of malfunction since high school. *Ronny just needs to refocus his priorities*, she told herself.

Nina had learned a trick or two since she had been married to Ronny. He taught her the art of stealing cars, and she turned out to have some natural ability in picking the right ones.

Nina pulled into the truck stop. The staple of early morning customers at the stop consisted of two types of people: the truckers and the seniors. The truckers, who had parked their rigs at the truck stop the previous night to avoid the frozen and icy roadways, were preparing to head back out on the road again. The senior citizens were all locals who went there for the cheap, generously sized breakfasts that the roadside eatery was known for.

Nina parked behind a white building in a spot that was a safe distance away from the other patrons. She scanned the lot and noticed a silver Honda sitting on the opposite side of where she was. *Must be the car.* She pulled down the visor and opened the vanity mirror. Her dishwater, blonde hair was frizzy, and the distinct wrinkles under her eyes made her look much older than her age. She reached in her purse and removed a small compact and lipstick case. She dabbed makeup on both sides of her face and rubbed it in to make her skin appear more vibrant. For the final touch, she traced her lips with a bright red shade of lipstick. Then she tussled with her hair until she was satisfied with how it looked. *Now*

*I'm ready to see my Ronny.* She got out of the car and slammed the door shut. After grabbing a quick look at herself in the driver's side mirror, she headed on foot toward the Honda.

Lucas watched Nina Trapp's white Taurus pull into the parking spot on the opposite side of the lot from him. He waited ten minutes for her slender figure to finally emerge. Lucas stepped out to greet her.

"Hi, Nina, Ronny's up the road," Lucas said.

"Why didn't he come with you? Nina snapped.

"He wasn't sure if you were followed. He wanted to make sure it was safe."

Lucas escorted Nina to the passenger side door of his car and opened it. After she got in, he shut the door. Then he walked around the car and hopped in on the driver's side.

"I was careful. Nobody knows I'm here."

*That's what I'm counting on.* "He wasn't sure. Ronald has run into a bit of bad luck as of late." *A lot of bad luck.*

"He taught me a lot," Nina said as she clipped her seatbelt.

*Obviously not enough.* Lucas started the engine and began driving. "We're going to go see him now. By the way, did you get rid of the cell phone that you used to call me?" Lucas looked at her and smiled.

Nina frowned. "Well, no, I still have it. It's turned off, though."

*Dumb fucking bitch.* "We can get rid of it when we see Ronny." Lucas flashed her an annoyed look.

"Sorry. I didn't think the police could track it." Nina shook her head.

Lucas grinned. "Don't worry, we will take care of everything in a few minutes."

"Don't tell Ronny. He would be disappointed." Nina dropped her head in disgust.

*How fucking pathetic.* "It will be our little secret." Lucas smiled again.

"Thanks."

"Not a problem. Consider me a friend." Lucas turned the car up a gravel road and stopped in front of a neglected farmhouse.

"Is he in there?" Nina pointed in the direction of the worn down structure.

"I told him to wait for us in the barn. Go on ahead. I'll catch up with you in a minute." Lucas grabbed his cell phone and pretended to make a call.

Before Lucas finished fake dialing a phone number, Nina was already out of the car and running in the direction of the barn.

*Stupid girl.* Lucas watched her walk through the barn door.

Nina burst through the barn door and called out, "Ronny! Where are you? I'm here, baby." She looked to her left and noticed a rickety ladder. "Ronny, you up there? Patrick is here with me."

Curiosity had gotten the best of her as she started to climb upward. She had only reached the second wrung when she felt a sharp pain shoot down the back of her neck.

"Ouch. What the fuck?"

Nina reached up and grasped the intruder of the assault. Before she could remove what had invaded her flesh, she lost her balance and fell backwards. She didn't even feel the sudden impact that her body made as it bounced off the cold surface. All she felt was an overpowering numbness. She was losing consciousness. Her vision was becoming blurred, but she was able to make out a man standing above her.

Lucas knelt down and smiled. "Nina, say hello to your husband for me."

Lucas inched closer to his victim. *Hmm, I guess people do die with their eyes open.* He reached out with a gloved hand and closed Nina Trapp's eyelids for the final time.

# Chapter 35

# Paralytic Promulgation

Kelli Jordan was doing her best to be useful, but finding the mutilated torso of Marissa Hodges was even too much for her to bear. She looked outside the small window and turned away in disgust. The media circus had received an anonymous tip about the dead woman and were already infesting the neighborhood. The ringleader of the event was none other than Ron Plesic. Kelli shook her head when she saw Ron, thinking, *He's the biggest leech of all.* She tried not to think about Ron Plesic and the other media people as she collected hair samples around the body.

Craig bent down and put a hand on Kelli's shoulder. "Hey, kiddo, you gonna be all right? I wanted to say sorry for not believing you on this."

Kelli forced a nervous smile. "I wouldn't have believed me, either. You see who's out there spewing his bullshit?" Kelli pointed out the window.

"Didn't take long for the pack to smell blood."

Craig helped Kelli to her feet and led her to the area where all the patrol units were parked. The two patrol units originally on the scene had multiplied ten-fold.

Kelli scanned the crowd. "Everybody is at this party."

"The chief will be coming. Almost a guarantee on that. Hey, just so you know, I won't be saying anything about that little angry outburst you had."

"It was sort of melodramatic of me. Just wanted to find her alive."

"I know you did."

"This killer goes to a lot of trouble to create the perfect setting. Don't you think?" Kelli asked.

"Maybe he gets off on it."

"There's something else," Kelli said.

"Nobody ever sees him," Craig said, guessing what she was about to say.

"Right. Not one fucking person." Kelli watched the news teams set up their equipment.

Craig scratched his head. "I got a few officers going door to door. Maybe they will have some luck."

"We're going to need some—that's for sure."

They walked back inside.

Kelli's portable radio squelched with activity. "30-58 from Dispatch," a male voice said.

"Go ahead, Dispatch," Kelli said.

"30-58, be advised that the chief is en route to the scene. He needs you and 30-53 to remain there until he arrives."

Kelli frowned. "10-4, Dispatch. Thanks for letting us know." She flashed her partner a worried look. "You were right. Think he's coming to take us off these cases?"

"Not quite yet. I'm sure the feds are breathing down on him

pretty hard. I know they really want to take over the Holden and Nesmith cases."

"I'm not sure they will do any better than us."

"Don't worry about it until it happens," Craig said.

A uniformed police supervisor approached them and said, "Hello, I'm Captain Bartley. We did a sweep of the area. Most of the people in the neighborhood didn't know our victim."

*Perfect target for a killer.* "Thanks for checking it out for us. According to her vehicle registration, she was only here a few months."

"We also looked for her missing parts, but we couldn't find them anywhere. I figured we would find a trail of blood outside the residence, but we didn't," Captain Bartley said with a grim look on his face.

*The maniac took them with him.* "Captain, thanks for keeping us informed," Kelli said.

"It's a strange murder, Detective Jordan. Very strange." Captain Bartley waved a cursory goodbye and returned to his team of officers.

Kelli's cell phone vibrated. She plucked it off her belt and flipped it open.

"Detective Jordan."

"Hey, Kelli, it's Kurt Delong. I need to talk to you and Craig right away."

"Kurt, there's been another murder. It's related to the Tahoe case." *Of course it is related.*

"Yes, I think Steve, the other coroner, will be handling the case you have there. I found something in the remains of the burn victim."

"What did you find?" Kelli asked.

"Not on the phone. Meet me at your office within the hour."

"Chief's supposed to show up soon, but it shouldn't take long," Kelli said as she watched the identification team sift through Marissa's remains.

"This is something big. Please meet me as soon as possible," Kurt urged.

"Give us a little time. We will be there," Kelli assured him.

"Will do. I'll see you there." Kurt hung up.

Kelli nudged Craig and whispered in his ear, "Kurt found something. Sounds like there's a major development with the Tahoe victim."

Craig's eyes widened. "What do you think it is?"

"I don't know, but I have a feeling it will link these two murders in some way."

"Let's hope so."

Craig and Kelli went back into the upstairs room to search for evidence. A few minutes later, the Chief of Marcona walked into the hallway and motioned for them to follow him outside.

"Kelli, Craig, let's talk out front. I see that ass Plesic is getting too close to my crime scene."

Once outside, the chief ranted about the unsolved murders and the fact that more murders kept happening. He said he was beginning to wonder if his department had the skills and resources to handle the situation. Kelli had a feeling Chief Roger Hendricks was about to give in to the feds. She hoped Kurt Delong had information that would help.

After the chief's spiel, Craig and Kelli knew without a

doubt that they were running on borrowed time. They hurried to their cars, anxious to meet with the medical examiner.

Kurt Delong was outside waiting for Kelli and Craig when they parked in front of the police department.

He walked up to them as they exited their cars and said, "Hey, I have something you two need to see. You're not going to believe it." He reached into his coat and took out a red folder and a marker.

Together, they all walked inside the station and entered a side office off the main corridor. Kelli closed the door behind them.

"Good news, I hope."

Kurt opened the folder, removed three photos, and spread them out on the desk. "Look closely at this area here." He circled the victim's throat in each of the three pictures.

Craig leaned over. "Looks like a piece of metal."

Kurt nodded. He pulled out a small plastic baggie. "Right. That's exactly what it is. It's actually the tip of a needle." Kurt handed the baggie over to Kelli.

Kelli held the bag up to the light. "How did this not burn up like most everything else?"

"It was thrust deep inside his throat before he burned. The metal also contains something else."

Kelli turned to Craig and pounded the desk once with her fist. "It's the drug, isn't it?"

"Traces of Propaganician were present," Kurt confirmed.

"You gotta be kidding!" Craig shook his head.

"I knew it. We got one killer for three, now possibly four victims." Kelli picked up one of the photos and analyzed it.

"Looks that way. I called the other coroner handling your latest victim. Told him to run blood samples for the drug." Kurt flipped to a page in the file. "Also, look at the Propaganician levels of your other two victims. Grant Nesmith and Shauna Holden were dead within thirty seconds of being exposed."

Kelli handed the photos back to Kurt. "Why go to all the trouble to create elaborate death scenes?" she asked.

Kurt looked up from the folder, winked at Kelli, and said, "Maybe this is the start of something bigger."

Craig put his feet up on the desk. "Doc, now you are sounding like her. We don't have any evidence supporting that."

Kelli shot her partner a frozen stare. "Well, we don't have any that disapproves it either."

Kurt stood up and opened the door. "I will check with Steve about the Hodges woman. I should know something in a couple days."

Kelli escorted Kurt back to his car as Craig retreated to his office.

"Thanks for the information. There has been too many dead ends in these cases. Now we may have something to go on," Kelli said.

Kurt smiled. "Your partner doesn't seem to think they are related."

"He likes things wrapped up in a neat little bow. Things out of the normal spectrum seem to make Craig a little nervous,"

Kelli joked.

"Ha! A little? I have to get going, but if I hear anything, I will be sure to give you a call."

"I will do the same."

Kelli backed away from the car and watched him leave. *Time for a little rest. It has been a long day.*

As Kelli was driving home, something on a roadside billboard caught her eye. She pulled the car to the curb and rushed out to get a better look at the event posted on the front. She focused her cell phone camera on the billboard. After snapping the picture, she got back into her car and drove home. She felt confident that the information on the billboard would lead her to the man responsible for creating the deadly drug.

# Chapter 36

# Contacting Valentine

Kelli Jordan stumbled out of her bedroom. Empty wine cooler bottles were scattered all over the kitchen counter, which explained why her head was pounding. She sat down at the kitchen table and picked up several articles about Dr. Samuel Longnecker that she had printed from the Internet. She got the doctor's name from the billboard she took a picture of on the previous night. It was advertising his upcoming conference on his experimental medications and treatments. *Shit, if anyone knows about our killer's drug, it's this guy.* She picked up one of the articles and read it.

**Bourne Hospital Ends Experimental Medication Program**

Bourne Hospital administrators have ended the experimental medication and treatment program of one of its staff doctors. The doctor was also fired. The experimental program at Bourne Hospital has resulted in injury and death, as well as numerous complaints and several lawsuits. A representative of Bourne Hospital announced that Dr. Samuel Longnecker is helping them to evaluate the safety of any future programs and is working to develop better oversight procedures and safety standards.

Kelli's heart was racing. *This is the break I have been looking for.* She jumped up from her seat, went over to her copy machine, and made several duplicates of the article. *It's a long shot, but maybe whoever they asked to resign is out for some revenge,* she thought. She searched the table, found an empty brown folder, and stuck the paperwork inside it. Then she returned to her bedroom.

Right as Kelli sat on her bed, she noticed the blinking light on the answering machine. She pushed the play button and listened to the message. It had something to do with the case. She grabbed a piece of paper and wrote down the caller's phone number. Then she hastily picked up the phone and returned the call.

"Hello, Dr. Alan Sanderson speaking," an older man with a distinguished voice answered.

"Dr. Sanderson, this is Marcona Police Homicide Detective Kelli Jordan. I just got your message."

"Ah, Detective Jordan, thank you for returning my call. I hope I'm not intruding by contacting you at home. Dr. Delong gave me your number."

"Sir, I appreciate your call." Kelli sat down on her bed.

"As I mentioned on your machine, I saw the nationwide forensics alert on Propaganician. I personally have worked several investigations where the drug was utilized."

"You're in Nebraska?" Kelli asked. *That's quite a distance.*

"Yes. The city of Valentine, to be precise."

"Doc, you had cases there?"

"Indeed, young lady, we did. Several murders, and even a few police officers were victims."

"I never heard anything about that," Kelli said. Usually the law enforcement network is excellent at posting alerts when police officers are murdered.

"It was kept quiet. The murders themselves were publicized, but anything mentioning the paralytic drug was not included."

"How can that be?" Kelli asked.

"The city officials didn't want to create a panic."

"Law enforcement should have every detail on something like this."

"Agreed. It should have been disseminated much better. The killer struck fast, and then he was gone."

"It just stopped—like that?" Kelli asked.

"Just as quickly as it started."

"Why would this fucking maniac just stop killing?"

"I have been wondering about that for several months," the doctor said.

"Now he's taken up a home here and is on a murdering spree."

"Detective, this killer used to mark his victims."

"Mark his victims? What do you mean?" Kelli asked.

"He would engrave a signature, or at least I thought it was a signature, into the bodies."

*Like a fucking autograph?* "Nothing like that so far. When you mean signature, what did it say?" Kelli asked.

"The phrase, "Death's Calling."

"What does it mean?"

"We never figured it out."

"Well it freaking means something." Kelli opened the top drawer of her dresser and slid out a pad of paper.

"We think it's a nickname that he calls himself."

"Sounds like a taunt or threat or something."

"That's what the lead detective thought," he said in a soft tone of voice.

"What is his name? Maybe we can compare notes. It would be helpful." Kelli readied her pen.

"His name was Brian Jeffers."

"Don't you mean is?" Kelli asked.

"Brian recently passed away. He was brutally gunned down in Colorado by a real unpleasant man named Ronald Trapp."

Kelli sprung to her feet. "What did you say?"

"I said a man named Ronald Trapp was responsible for his death."

"Dr. Sanderson, that individual is possibly one of our dead victims here."

"Why would Trapp come to your town?"

"Believe me, we have been asking ourselves that same question."

"That's very strange. It doesn't make a lot of sense."

"Unless, our cases happen to be related, which I'm thinking they are?"

"Detective, how did Trapp die?"

Kelli wasn't sure if she should share information about the investigation, but the chief did tell her and Craig to use any resources available to solve the murders, so she decided to answer Dr. Sanderson's question.

"The killer shoved Propaganician down Trapp's throat, threw him into a truck, and then set the vehicle on fire."

"This sounds like the same killer, Detective. Just like him."

Kelli couldn't disagree. "So Brian Jeffers gets murdered by Trapp. Then this man who calls himself Lucas whacks Trapp. Almost makes you think he sent Trapp after Jeffers."

"Indeed, it almost does," Dr. Sanderson agreed.

"Doc, question for you?"

"Ask away."

"How did you find out about Brian Jeffers being murdered? Internet, the Police Network System, or local media?"

"I heard it from a few police officers in town. There was an article in the Desoto Valley paper as well."

"Do you know why he left Valentine?" Kelli pried.

Dr. Sanderson hesitated. "Brian's wife and eldest daughter were the last two murdered by the killer. He couldn't stay there anymore, so he picked up and moved to Colorado."

*Too much grief for anyone to take,* Kelli thought. *Maybe his former chief can help out with some information.* "You wouldn't happen to know the chief of police's phone number, would you?"

"Of course. We have been friends a long time."

"You wouldn't mind giving it to me, would you?"

"Not at all. You have a pen?

After Dr. Sanderson gave Kelli the phone number, she asked if he would send the death investigation reports to Kurt Delong. He was more than happy to oblige. He indicated the paperwork would be there later that day.

Kelli searched the Internet for the Desoto Valley Police website. Within seconds, the search engine provided a link. She clicked it. The site loaded almost instantly. After studying the site for a few minutes, she found the headline about the ambush shooting.

Kelli peeked over at her notepad where she had written down the phone number for Valentine's chief. She keyed the number into her phone. Her call was transferred to a voice mailbox system that requested her name and number, which she left accordingly. Kelli also added a little message that the Valentine police chief wouldn't ignore. After she hung up, she leaned back in her chair and waited. *There will be a return call. It is just a matter of time.*

# Chapter 37

# Discovering Chief Jeffers

---

Brian Jeffers was lounging on his sofa, trying to relax a little. Sleep hadn't been on his agenda, primarily because he was anticipating the results of the blood found on the fifty-cent piece. *Jake should have something today.* Brian forced himself to get up and grab the bottle of pain medication off the kitchen counter. He took off the lid and forced down a couple of the horse pills.

Just as Brian started to sit down, he heard a chat message alert. He went to his office, sat down at the computer, and checked the message. Then he requested a video chat with the person who had messaged him. Seconds later, Valentine Chief of Police Ralph Anderson appeared on the screen. Brian thought it was odd that the man was contacting him, but he felt cooped up in the house, so he welcomed any contact with the outside world.

"You are looking old," Brian joked.

"Okay, you go ahead and deal with these rookie cops and we'll see how old you look," Ralph said.

"Your message said it was urgent."

"I received a call today from a homicide investigator in

North Dakota."

"What's going on?"

"She left me a message. You're not going to believe what it was."

Brian shrugged. "Enlighten me, wise one."

"Death's Calling were her exact words. He's in their town. Has been for about a week or so," Ralph said.

Brian leaned closer to the camera. "What the fuck! How many dead this time?"

"At least three so far. There might be a fourth. You're not gonna believe who one of them was. Ronald Trapp may have been burned alive."

Brian gritted his teeth. "He killed that son of a bitch?"

"It appears so. This investigator who called me thinks Trapp was sent to kill you, and then he was removed from the picture."

"She's right. Ronald was too stupid to be the head of anything more elaborate than a circle jerk," Brian said. The pain in his chest doubled.

"You're right about that. But Brian, Death's Calling wanted him dead for some reason."

"He kills everybody. You and I both know that." Brian rubbed his chin.

"This Kelli Jordan also wanted to talk to you, if you were still alive." Ralph grinned.

Sounds like this girl's smart. She doesn't think Trapp killed me?"

"I don't think the fake blurb on the websites or newspapers convinced her. That's the kind of woman this department needs here."

"Did she say anything else?"

"She did. Mentioned something about blood evidence left at the scene of one murder."

Brian stared hard at the camera. "Blood evidence?" *Two possible pieces of evidence with blood on them.*

"Do you want me to call her back and confirm your death, or would you like to talk with her?" Ralph asked with a smile on his face.

"No, I think maybe we both can help each other."

"I bet you can help her. She sounds like an attractive woman."

"Get your mind out of the gutter. If your wife only knew what a pervert you are." Brian laughed.

"Believe me, she knows. Yep, she knows."

"Hey, it was great to hear from you, Ralph. I don't get out often."

"I do wish you hadn't left. Too many kids working here now," Ralph said with a disgusted look on his face.

"Memories, buddy. Too many of them."

"I understand. Keep me in the loop. I will send you an email attachment with the information she sent me."

"Thanks. Maybe when we catch this bastard we can get a drink or two. Your dime of course." Brian smiled.

"Of course. I wouldn't have it any other way."

Brian turned off the webcam and waited for the email from his former mentor. It arrived a few minutes later. It contained several attachments. One was a news article about Bourne Hospital. He remembered that hospital from his investigation of Death's Calling. *Bourne Hospital Administration. That was on the bottom of the wheelchair in August Dellano's hotel room.* Death's Calling had left the device in the dead man's room. Further investigation to find where it originated from resulted in nothing.

Brian read through the entire story, convinced there was a connection. He scrolled to the woman's contact information and picked up his cell phone.

Kelli was perched at her desk in her cubicle, finishing the last bite of her bagel, when the office phone rang.

She picked up the phone. "Detective Jordan speaking."

"Hello. I hear you're looking for Brian Jeffers," a deep male voice said.

*Could this be him?* "You sound pretty good for someone who is supposed to be dead," Kelli teased.

"I will take that as a compliment, I guess." Brian laughed.

*He has a sense of humor. That's always nice.* "Glad to see you have recovered," Kelli said as she scribbled on her memo pad.

"Not fully, but I'm getting close."

"So, did you have a chance to review the attachments?" Kelli asked.

"I did. Ralph forwarded them to me. Oh, you sort of freaked him out with your message."

*It got results.* "Sorry, I figured he would return my call if I got his attention."

"You definitely got his attention. You got mine, too."

"So, what do you think?"

"I'm very interested in your blood evidence."

*I think he believes me.* "I'm still waiting for the results." Kelli typed Brian's full name into the police database. *I need to know more about this guy.*

"Detective Jordan?"

"Call me Kelli."

"Okay, Kelli. Call me Brian. The killer left evidence at my house as well . . . " Brian's voice weakened when he said, " . . . after he killed my family."

Kelli almost felt guilty. She was looking up background information on him while he was sharing such a painful piece of his life with her. "I'm sorry. I heard about the tragedy."

"Kelli, the article about the Bourne Hospital Administration is a key—at least I think it is."

"Yeah, I fucking got lucky stumbling upon it."

"Good that you did. It's a familiar name. We found a wheelchair at one of the murders labeled with it."

"Not to be nosy, but what happened with that lead in your case?"

"We thought it was stolen. The people at the hospital were less than helpful."

"They didn't even think it was strange?" Kelli asked.

"Believe me, I thought it was fucked up, too. Hey, I'm coming up with one of my brilliant ideas?"

"Brilliant?" Kelli asked as playfully as she could muster while simultaneously reading the on-screen information about Chief Brian Jeffers.

"Okay, maybe just a good idea."

"Let's hear it," Kelli said as she looked over a list of awards Brian had in his service file. She was impressed.

"Since I'm presumed dead, maybe you can research that lead with Dr. Samuel Longnecker?"

"I was thinking the same thing. If anybody knows something about Bourne Hospital, it would be him."

"If the killer worked there, Longnecker should know who he is," Brian said.

"I'm pretty sure Dr. Longnecker knows him. The article said Bourne Hospital fired the doctor who was treating people with experimental medications, and Dr. Longnecker works with experimental medicine, according to the billboard. Then there's the Bourne marking on the wheelchair at the crime scene. There's so many links. They must know each other," Kelli said.

"He's the man to talk to."

"My partner and I will check it out."

"Do that. Let me know what you find. I'm hoping to get the info back on this piece of evidence I have," Brian said.

"You know, this Samuel Longnecker could be on the killer's target list, if we're right." Kelli said.

"Kelli, when the killer left after the first murders, he took a police badge. It was put out on the Police Identification Network, but that was several months ago, and by now, most people have forgotten about it."

"Gotcha. I will keep my eyes out."

"He's killed several police officers. Just keep that in mind," Brian cautioned Kelli.

"Will do. Get yourself well so that you can give us a hand

catching this fucker."

Brian laughed. "That's what I'm hoping. I will keep you posted if I find anything that can help. "

"Okay, same here," Kelli said

"Thanks for including me in this."

"Welcome!" Kelli said. Then she hung up the phone.

# Chapter 38

# Diary of a Peasant

---

Lucas opened the container and gazed at his newest treasure. *Smaller than a fist.* He thrust both gloved hands inside and removed it with the utmost care. He brought the organ to the kitchen sink and rinsed it until all the loose blood was cleansed from its surface. *Now Ronald and Nina Trapp are both in my collection of masterpieces.* He put his new prize into a plastic baggie and zipped it closed. Then he washed his hands and bleached the sink. *No trace of the blood.* He peeked down at his watch. It was time to prepare. Diary of a Peasant would begin in less than two hours. *Hopefully Samuel will use the ticket I gave him.*

Lucas took the stairs up to his work area and stowed Nina Trapp's addition in its glass prison. Then he peeked at the aquarium and envisioned what it would be holding in a just a few more days. His lip curled into a gruesome smile. He closed the area and returned to his room. The idea of seeing Samuel Longnecker again sent a cool rush throughout his body. With much excitement, he sorted through the tools he needed to carry out his deadly agenda.

Samuel Longnecker was sitting at the table, landlocked between two of his biggest supporters. Sitting on his left side was sixty-three-year-old Wallace Meredith. Wallace was the silver-haired director of Marcona General Hospital and the former board administrator at Bourne Hospital. Sitting on his right side was thirty-nine-year-old Vanessa Triton. She was the CEO of Braxton Pharmaceuticals and Samuel's on-call mistress. Samuel hadn't seen the girl from the hotel. He figured she had probably checked out. *Oh well. Vanessa is here. That is better than nothing.*

Samuel took a healthy drink of his Chardonnay before continuing with the bland conversation, which had been going on since the beginning of dinner.

"Wallace, the price of medications needs to stay where it is. The market for high-priced, generic prescriptions is utterly outrageous," Samuel said.

Wallace smiled. "The industry will keep raising prices. That's how this wonderful economic system works. Learn to live with it."

"I still have a belief that we do this job for a purpose." Samuel threw his dinner napkin in the middle of the table and stood up.

"Oh, come on. You're going to leave because of a little disagreement?" Wallace eyed Samuel in disbelief.

"Not at all. I have another engagement to attend. I will give you a ring tomorrow."

Wallace stood up and offered his hand. "All right, no more about that for now. We will talk tomorrow in regards to how the conference itinerary will go. Take it easy and, Samuel, have a wonderful time this evening."

Samuel walked away from the table without looking in Vanessa's direction. He passed through an adjoining tunnel and discovered the line for the night's entertainment was of considerable length. Ready for the time of his life, he reached into his tuxedo breast pocket and fished out his lone admission slip to the event.

Lucas arrived at the auditorium and watched the side door fill with anxious patrons. His and Samuel's tickets were in the same section. He watched the entrance, waiting for Samuel to pass through. The steady flow of people continued for several minutes. Finally, Lucas recognized the pronounced limp of his former mentor. *Thin man has a potbelly.*

Lucas unconsciously shrunk back into his chair, even though it would have been near impossible for Samuel to see him. He gripped the plastic syringe, despite the fact that he had no intentions of using it that night. After all, he hadn't spent all that time preparing just to experience simple instant gratification. At that moment, he was only there to study his prey. The main attraction was still a few days away. He snapped the cap back on the needle and concentrated on watching the play.

When the play ended, Samuel stood up and headed for

the exit. Lucas eased out of his chair and hustled to a safe distance behind him. Samuel ended up in the massive parking lot. Lucas made sure not to lose him in the maze of expensive vehicles. Samuel opened the door to the dark-colored sedan and drove out of the lot. Lucas noted the license plate as he watched the car drive off. He reached up to his neckline and felt the gold pendant. A crooked smile creased his lips as he walked in the frozen night air. *It is all coming together. Within thirty-six hours, Samuel Longnecker will have a permanent home in my collection of masterpieces.*

# Chapter 39

# One Piece of the Puzzle

Jake Moreno called Brian Jeffers and asked him to stop by his office. Tricia Stonehouse insisted on driving Brian and wouldn't take no for an answer. Brian truly believed she was one of the only people he could trust.

Tricia peeked over at Brian and said, "Hey, you haven't said anything since I picked you up."

Brian managed a weak smile. "Just thinking. Sorry. I'm not great company."

"I figured it was just me," Tricia said. She gave him a wink.

"It's not." Brian changed the subject. "Jake said to pull around the back. He will be waiting there." Brian pointed to the side street.

Tricia turned into the rear parking lot and parked.

Jake Moreno was already waiting at the back of the storage dock. He approached the passenger side of the car and opened Brian's door.

"Take it easy," Jake said. He motioned for Tricia to get on Brian's other side.

"You seem a little worse than last time?"

"Just tired—that's all." Brian tried to stay on his feet. *Fucking medications making me zombie-like.*

Jake and Tricia escorted Brian into the building, moving at a slow pace to accommodate for the fact that he was feeling far from his best. It took them a few minutes to reach Jake's office.

Jake let go of Brian once they got inside and said, "Sit down and relax. I will be back in a few. You're not going to believe what I found."

Tricia and Brian made themselves comfortable.

Jake returned with two yellow envelopes. "Take a look at these," Jake said as he held the envelopes out to Brian.

Brian's hands trembled as he lifted the edge of the first envelope. He stared at the charts and printouts. There were three names highlighted in yellow. The word, DECEASED, was written next to each name. Brian didn't recognize two of the names, but he did recognize the third name, August Dellano, which reminded him of the killings in Valentine.

August Dellano was a fat Italian restaurant owner who was found tortured and mutilated in his hotel room. Brian still clearly remembered the river of blood that surrounded the bloated man's body. He almost got sick again just thinking about it. *I remember now. The coin originally belonged to that August bastard.* Brian handed the paperwork to Tricia.

Jake had a solemn look on his face as he said, "The first person was a woman named Angela Deeds. The medical examiner reports I brought up listed a gunshot wound as a cause of death. There is something strange in her lab work. Actually, all three of the lab reports."

Brian knew what Jake was going to say, so he went ahead and said it himself. "A paralytic drug named Propaganician was in their system. Wasn't it?" He already knew the answer.

Jake's eyes widened. "How did you know?"

"Most of his victims were injected with it before they were mutilated." Brian shook his head.

Tricia Stonehouse set down the paperwork. "This sicko injected them first?"

"That's his method of operation. He injects them, watches them die, and then displays them," Brian said as he wrung his hands together.

Jake pointed at the second envelope. "Take a look at that one."

Brian undid the clasp and pulled out the lone sheet of paper. He looked at the results. His pulse began increasing in speed, and the quicker it got, the more the pain in his chest subsided. "What the fuck is this?" Brian asked.

Jake sported a little grin. "That, my friend, is your killer's DNA. I was hoping to get something over the fax before you guys got here, but the database appears to be taking too long."

"What database are you talking about?" Brian perked up in his seat.

"When I saw the paralytic drug parallels in the victims, I got to thinking about state board licensing and the blood testing required by hiring entities of medical centers."

"For physicians, you mean?" Brian asked.

"Precisely, for physicians."

Brian shot up from the chair, almost forgetting how weak

he was feeling. "The asshole is on file?

"If he worked anywhere in the states," Jake said.

*I got you now.* Brian pumped his fist in the air. "Finally, something to identify him."

Jake looked at Brian and Tricia. "Once we get something back, you two send it out everywhere you can think of."

Tricia shook her head in agreement. "I can get it on the wire within the hour."

Brian was already miles away in his own thoughts. *I'm going to go wherever you are, Death's Calling—wherever you are.*

Brian kept thinking about how close he was to finding the man that murdered his wife and daughter. He wouldn't rest until the killer was buried deep beneath the earth.

# Chapter 40

# Dr. Lucas Calling

Kelli Jordan called Samuel Longnecker's publicist to find out where he was staying. After a debated discussion, the woman finally gave up the doctor's location. Kelli left Craig Berte a message telling him she was heading to Jos Glades Hotel to see Samuel and that he should meet her there as soon as possible.

The drive to Jos Glades Hotel was uneventful, and because Kelli was heavy on the gas pedal, she arrived in practically no time at all. She turned into the long driveway and was astonished when she saw the humongous building. She waved away the valet attendant without stopping the car. When she reached the parking lot, she saw Craig standing outside his car, smoking a cigar. *Shit, how fast was he going?* She pulled up next to him and stepped out of the car.

"Hey, Craig, you better not throw that on the ground. The staff will probably have you shot," Kelli joked as she lit her own cigarette.

"Yeah, what the fuck ever." Craig snickered.

"Samuel's publicist said he is in room 716." Kelli looked up at the structure.

Craig threw his cigarette on the ground and then looked at Kelli with a mischievous smirk on his face. "Don't want to keep Samuel waiting, do we?"

"Of course not." Kelli fieldstripped her cigarette and shoved the remains in her coat pocket.

Kelli and Craig walked up to the front of the hotel and were greeted by a man in a charcoal suit. They flashed their badges at him.

"I'm Detective Jordan. This is Detective Berte. We're here to see one of your guests. His name is Dr. Samuel Longnecker."

The man smiled warmly. "Hello, I'm Pierce Rottman. I'm the day manager at Jos Glades. Dr. Longnecker's assistant told us you would be coming."

*News travels fast*, Kelli thought. "Can you escort us to his room?"

"Follow me." Pierce opened the doors to the foyer.

Kelli almost gasped as she walked through the magnificent interior. There were two large, gold water fountains on each side of the marble covered lobby. One appeared to be a standard style, but the other was something a little different. Kelli stared at several people who were lined up in front of the fountain, each holding something in their hands. It took her a few seconds to realize what the guests were doing. The fountain was similar to something found at weddings, but on a much grander scale. The patrons were filling their silver goblets with the transparent liquid that was flowing out of fountain's several spout-like extensions.

The hotel manager noticed that Kelli was intrigued, so he offered an explanation. "A little something for people who enjoy the finer things in life."

*What a pretentious asshole.* "Definitely finer—"

"—When I make my first million, maybe I will come back here," Craig said, interrupting Kelli before something crude came out of her mouth.

Pierce Rottman ignored the comment. He withdrew a plastic key card from the breast pocket on his jacket and waved it in front of a small monitor. The elevator doors opened. The three of them stepped inside. The ride to the seventh floor was quiet, except for the electronic voice announcing each floor.

Craig leaned in close to Kelli and whispered, "I would go fucking nuts if I had to listen to that all the way to the sixtieth floor."

Kelli just shook her head.

When they reached the seventh floor, the elevator doors opened. They exited the elevator and followed Pierce down the hall to room 716. Pierce tapped on the door. A few seconds later, the semi-thin Dr. Samuel Longnecker came to the entryway. He was dressed in a forest green cardigan sweater and tan khakis.

"Sir, these are Officers Berte and Jordan," Pierce said.

Kelli smiled. "Actually, we are homicide investigators."

"Megan told me you were coming to talk to me." Samuel motioned for them to come inside. "Pierce, thanks for bringing them up here. I will call the front desk when I need a lift to my dinner engagement."

"Very well, Sir," Pierce said. He smiled at Samuel and snubbed the two investigators before exiting the room.

Samuel shut the door and pulled out two chairs from the buffet table for the detectives and one for himself. "So, what may I help you with, Detectives?"

Kelli opened her briefcase and pulled out two folders. "Sir, there has been a recent outbreak of murders in this city. In these murders that I'm referring to, Propaganician was used."

Samuel poured himself a glass of wine. "The drug is widely distributed through medical surplus companies. What makes you believe I would know anything?"

"You are the founder of this experimental drug, aren't you?" Kelli asked.

"Why, of course, but you already knew that. There's something else you're not telling me."

Kelli slid the article in front of Samuel. "This is why."

Samuel picked up the paper and skimmed it over. "This is over fifteen years old. All of a sudden you think some former employee of Bourne Hospital is using this drug to exact revenge?" Samuel slid the paper back to Kelli.

"That's what we think." Kelli said with a cold tone of voice. She shot Craig a look, silently pleading for him to step in.

Craig remained silent, but nodded his head in agreement.

*Can't blame him for not saying anything*, Kelly thought. *It does sound crazy.*

"Detective, the odds of that being the case are phenomenal. Do you have any more evidence, other than an old article clip?" Samuel pointed at the article.

Kelli hesitated. "Dr. Longnecker, this isn't the first time that this has happened." She handed him the other folder.

"More cases?" Samuel asked. He opened the second

folder and flipped through the color photos. He covered his mouth in response to the gruesome scenes.

"These cases are from a place called Valentine. Several dead there as well. The one thing in common, though, is the use of Propaganician," Kelli said.

Samuel Longnecker's face turned ashen as he nervously thumbed through the entire file. "The marking on each of the victims is familiar to me—very familiar." Samuel finished his wine while staring at the pictures, trying to place where he had seen the markings before.

Craig leaned in close to Kelli and whispered, "He knows who it is."

"Familiar how, Dr. Longnecker?" Kelli opened her notepad.

"I'm not sure. Wait . . . is that . . . .Oh no . . . The engravings are of a man's name." Samuel tapped the pictures of Sarah and Melissa Jeffers.

"A man's name?" Kelli asked as she scribbled in her notepad.

Samuel slowly lifted his head. "He was once a good friend . . . until we parted company." Samuel Longnecker ran his fingers along the pictures. "His name was Lucas Michael Calling. The other doctors that worked with him used to call him Death's Calling."

Craig rushed out the door.

"Sir, what happened at the hospital? Why did they call him Death's Calling? Why did he start killing people?" Kelli asked. She poised her pen, ready to write down whatever Samuel said next.

Samuel shakily grabbed at the wine bottle and filled his

glass a second time. "The hospital was having complications with the formula of the paralytic drug."

"Yes, I read in the article that there were a few deaths from the experimental medications," Kelli said.

Samuel guzzled down the alcohol. "Detective, not just a few people—many died before the drug was finally perfected. Many thought Lucas was subjecting people to a stronger version of the original compound. That's why, whenever Lucas got a new test subject, some of the staff would joke, 'Watch out, Death's Calling again.'"

"It wasn't just him, was it?"

"I guess there's no point in hiding from the truth now. It was partially my fault," Samuel admitted.

"But they fired him instead of you, didn't they?"

"He was the young hotshot who broke protocols all the time. The medical facility thought it was best to use him as the scapegoat."

"Now he blames you, and the murders are his way of getting even." Kelli raised a brow.

Tears formed in Samuel's eyes. "I wouldn't have thought he was capable."

"Those pictures should tell you something else. I do wonder something, though."

Samuel wiped the wetness from his face. "Excuse me, what would that be?"

"I want to know if those murders were just a precursor for something larger." Kelli ripped the folder from Samuel's hands and put it back into her briefcase.

Samuel had a dumbfounded look on his face as he asked,

"What could that be?"

Kelli stood up and walked toward the exit. Before she left, she turned and said, "If he is holding you responsible for his firing and being made the scapegoat for the failed medical treatments, it would make sense for you to be on his list. More so than any of the other people in this folder." Kelli tapped the briefcase.

Kelli opened the door and walked out, leaving Dr. Samuel Longnecker time to reflect on the past and the countless deaths that he could have prevented.

# Chapter 41

# Universes Collide

Brian Jeffers grabbed his clothes from the closet and shoved them in the nylon garment bag. *Should be all I need.* He estimated that the drive from Desoto Valley to his destination would take twelve hours at best. The estimation included time out for refueling and one quick food break. He walked over to his dresser, opened the top drawer, reached in, and removed the stun gun he had purchased from the local military surplus store. He opened the back compartment and replaced the batteries. Then he flipped on the stun gun's power switch. A crackling noise sounded and blue sparks flowed from one steel prong to another. Satisfied that it was working properly, he clicked the weapon off and placed it gently in his carry-on bag. He snatched his car keys from the table and put on his winter coat. Brian was ready to walk out the door when he heard the high-pitched sound of the fax machine. He opened the door to the office and looked at the incoming fax. He recognized the number sending the transmission.

*What have you got for me, Jake?* Brian wondered as he watched a picture emerge from the fax machine. He turned it over and stared at the photo. Then he haphazardly folded the paper and stuffed it inside his coat pocket. He stomped out of the office, picked up his bags, and walked out of the house, slamming the front door behind him. His mind felt like it was spinning as he walked to the car and loaded his bags in the trunk. He hopped in the driver's seat and started the engine. As he shifted the car into gear, tears began to stream down his face. *Time to meet you face to face.*

Kelli Jordan stopped in front of Craig Berte's cubicle and flashed him a smile. "Everything done?" she asked.

"Pretty much. The all-points bulletin is almost out everywhere. The picture we have is from his Nebraska driver's license." Craig handed her the color photo.

Kelli looked at the picture and said, "What a cliché."

Craig looked at Kelli quizzically. "What cliché?"

"The guy's name is Patrick Vain? Come on, look at the guy. Movie star looks and that smile—of course his alias would be something close to that." She crammed the picture in a folder.

"Of course, why didn't my old ass think of that?" Craig teased.

"Hmm, couldn't tell ya. Does the local news have it yet?"

"With bloodsucking Ron Plesic on the job, of course they do," Craig said as he typed on the keyboard. "By the way, what happened after I left the hotel room?"

"Let's just say that I gave Dr. Longnecker something to think about."

"Do you think Lucas will really come after him?" Craig asked.

"I'm counting on it. I have a few undercover officers keeping an eye on Longnecker. If Lucas decides to go after him, they will be ready."

"Did you bother to tell Longnecker?" Craig asked.

"Not yet. The guys on the detail will be an obvious hint to him once he tries to go fifty feet from the hotel. "

"You're a bad girl. That guy is probably scared to death about now."

"Like I said, he might be rethinking a few things."

"Well, you might want to let Chief know in case something goes fucking haywire."

"I already sent him a quick update, so we should be good," Kelli said. She gave him a thumbs-up. Then she abruptly turned to walk away, and when she did, she almost collided with Andrew Ball.

"Geesh, slow down. We need to talk," Andrew said.

"Sure. You got the results back on the money clip, didn't you?"

Andrew smiled. "Of course I did. Where's your partner?"

Kelli held out her hand. "Now, please."

Andrew pulled a piece of paper out of the green folder he was holding and handed it to her. "Okay, two blood types are on that sheet. The murdered girl at the scene and a man named—"

"—Lucas Calling." Kelli winked.

"When did you find out?" Andrew asked with a deflated look on his face.

"Actually, just today. This psycho killed in the same way a few states over."

"Sorry I couldn't get the results to you quicker," Andrew apologized.

"Every little bit helps. Besides, you gave it to me now," Kelli said as she gently placed her hand on his arm.

Andrew walked toward the lobby. Kelli's eyes followed him until he was out of sight. *What a hottie, and he is so sweet,* Kelli thought to herself. She couldn't help but smile.

Kelli returned to her desk to run Dr. Lucas Calling's name through the police database. She spent several hours trying to find anything on the name, but the information network kept coming up with nothing. She even ran the alias, but that ended in failure as well. The phone on her desk buzzed, giving her a break from the frustration of finding nothing.

"Detective Jordan. How can I help you?"

"Kelli, it's Brian Jeffers. I need to speak with you."

"Where are you?" She didn't recognize the number on the caller identification system.

"On a cell phone. I'm about a hundred miles away."

"You're on the way here?" Kelli asked.

"I need to be there. I got the results back on my evidence." Brian's voice softened. "I know the identity of the man who killed my family."

"Brian, we know too. Our testing on the money clip proved my hunch was right."

"Did you talk to that Longnecker person?" Brian asked.

"Bastard used to work with him. They were like best fucking friends or something."

"You think Longnecker is a target now?"

Kelli chuckled. "Great minds do think alike. I got a few plainclothes guys on him. I'm sure if Lucas Calling shows up, he will really be surprised.

"Good idea. Does the local news have his picture out yet?"

"Got it out early this afternoon. They have been showing it every fifteen minutes since."

"It's just a matter of time now," Brian said.

Kelli could sense something else was wrong. She really didn't know Brian Jeffers well, but his distant demeanor did sort of worry her.

"So you're coming here? Maybe that's not such a great idea. You do have a lot invested in this manhunt." She almost bit her lip, knowing Brian had been through a nightmare. Her asking him to back off was probably not one of her brightest moves.

"I'll stay out of the way. I promise. Besides, I had my former chief talk to yours, and he's okay with it."

"Really?" Kelli knew Chief Hendricks didn't like anyone playing in his backyard.

"No, not really. He bitched a little, but I gave him my word that I would be a good boy. Kelli, this is just something I have to do. Closure to this horrible reality is all I want," Brian said in a calm yet almost eerie tone.

Kelli backed off. "So, you got somewhere to stay?"

"A small hotel in town."

"Where?" Kelli asked.

"I'll have to look. I don't remember the name offhand," Brian lied.

"Brian, I have an extra room in my house, if you want," Kelli offered.

"No, I wouldn't want to get my ass beat by a jealous husband or boyfriend."

Kelli felt herself blush. "No jealous husband or boyfriend to worry about. Just good ole me and my empty house. So, what do you say? It's not every day that I invite a guy over."

Brian laughed. "I don't want to impose on you."

"You aren't. It would also give us a chance to talk about the case." She unconsciously twirled the phone cord around her finger.

"Are you sure?" Brian asked.

"It's no problem. Trust me."

"Well, I will only accept if you let me make dinner for you."

Kelli smiled. "It's a deal, but nothing too spicy."

"Okay, no spicy stuff for the girl," Brian said with a soft laugh.

Kelli gave him her address before they ended the call. After she hung up, she picked up her briefcase and exited the building. The mixture of blowing snow, accompanied with burnt out streetlights, made it so she didn't see the red Honda that was closing in on her. She fumbled with her keys.

Lucas clenched his teeth as he gripped the steering wheel. He revved the motor and flipped on the vehicle's high beams. Kelli turned to face the lights.

Lucas was filled with rage. *This is the bitch who is trying to ruin everything.* He shifted the car into a higher gear and slammed his foot on the accelerator. *Goodbye, Detective.*

Kelli saw the car bearing down on her. She tried to leap

out of the way, but it was too late. The Honda's front bumper hit her with such force that it threw her body up into the air. The speed and impact of the fall back down caused her body to bounce helplessly along the pavement, each jarring blow ripping flesh from bone, until she finally came to rest at the foot of a snow pile.

Lucas pulled up next to Kelli and watched her blood seep onto the wet surface. *She will be dead soon.* He smiled with delight as he gazed into her fading eyes. He turned the corner and took one final look back at Kelli Jordan before he left the area. *One problem out of the way. One more to go.*

# Chapter 42

# Hiding in Plain Sight

Brian Jeffers studied the paper, double-checking to make sure he was at the right house. *This is the address.* He pulled down the visor and looked at the built-in digital clock. He had been waiting for two hours. The Marcona Police Department was only ten minutes away. He assumed his host would have made it home already. He picked up his cell phone and dialed Kelli's number. After five rings, the voice mail system kicked in. He left a quick message and hung up.

*Maybe she is stuck at work.* Brian knew all too well how that could happen. On several occasions, his plans with his girls were ruined when he was called in for a case. He picked up the map and searched for the police department's address. After he found the address and mapped his route, he pulled the car away from the curb and headed in that direction.

Lucas slid the closet door open and rummaged through several plastic bags. *This is it.* He untied one of the bags and removed several pieces of worn clothing. Then he stripped down and put on the worn garments. He looked at himself in the mirror and thought, *nobody will even know*. He retreated to the closet and found the brass-handled walking stick. If he was going to play the part, he needed to look convincing to people around him. *Just one final touch.* He stopped in front of the brown dresser, opened the bottom drawer, and picked through the mass of hairpieces until he found the right one. He put the hairpiece on and adjusted it. He returned to the mirror and was amazed at his own brilliance. *Just what the doctor ordered.*

Lucas was aware of the extra security measures Kelli Jordan had taken to protect Samuel, so he knew he had to execute his plan without a single flaw. He picked up two handguns and hid them under his oversized shirt. *Just in case.* The police and media were sure to be all over the hit and run, especially since it involved one of their police detectives. Lucas hurried out the door, ready to pay his respects to the late Kelli Jordan.

Brian Jeffers turned up the side street adjacent to Marcona Police Department. A uniformed police officer stopped him and said, "Sir, you can't come this way."

Brian opened his coat and flashed his credentials. "What's going on?"

The officer leaned inside the car and inspected Brian's badge and identification. "Chief, you're a long way from home. Why are you here?"

Brian smiled. "I was supposed to meet somebody at your department."

"Sir, who are you looking for?"

"Detective Kelli Jordan."

The young patrolman's eyes widened and the color drained out of his face. "Chief, there was an accident—"

"—I see that. If you can tell me where the Detective is—"

"—Sir, you don't understand. She was in the accident."

"What!"

"Hit and run Chief . . . nobody around when it happened." The patrol officer leaned on Brian's window. "A drunk driver, Sir. That's what it looks like right now."

Brian shook his head. "Is she gonna make it?"

The patrol officer bowed his head. "It doesn't look like it, Sir."

A wave of emotions flooded though Brian. He didn't like the timing of the accident. Since Lucas was somewhere in town, he had a bad feeling about what had happened.

"Where's her partner?" Brian asked.

"Detective Berte is up there with the traffic investigator." The patrol officer pointed in the direction of the accident.

"Radio him. Tell him I need to speak with him."

"Of course, Sir."

A few minutes later, the middle-aged form of Craig Berte walked up to Brian. His coat and pants were covered in blood. "Chief Jeffers?"

Brian stepped out of the car. "Yes. You Kelli's partner?"

"Yes. They paged me when the ambulance got here."

"Did she tell you I was coming into town?" Brian asked. He found himself staring at the bloodstains.

"No, I just found out."

"Is she going to make it?"

"They transported her to Marcona General. They said they got her stabilized, but that's all I know."

Brian leaned up against the car. "The officer said it was a hit and run?"

"Looks like a fucking drunk ran her down in the middle of the fucking street."

"Nobody saw it happen?" Brian asked.

Craig shook his head in disgust. "Not a word from anyone as of yet."

"How about the video? Anything from that?" Brian didn't want to overstep his bounds, but he hadn't believed in bad luck since the day he found his family murdered.

"No video. The cameras aim toward the police station, not away."

Brian glanced at the police station's front entrance. "Are they hidden, or does the general public know they are being recorded?"

"The cameras are all in the foyer, positioned to capture incoming visitors." Craig used his hands to illustrate.

"Hmm, I don't like the timing of all this."

Craig puffed on his cigar. "You don't think a drunk was responsible for the accident?"

Fuck no. "I don't think so." Brian folded his arms over his chest. "I called her earlier and told her about the evidence I had collected. It matched your killer. I wonder if Lucas was watching her. It's not uncommon for his method of operation," Brian said.

"I read those reports from Valentine. Why would he go after Kelli?"

"Because she exposed him before he could finish what he came to do."

"The Longnecker guy, right?" Craig asked.

Brian nodded his head. "No doubt he is infuriated about that."

"So he goes after Kelli for revenge?" Craig bowed his head. "You know, the bastard's good as caught anyway. All the news stations and law enforcement agencies for the next three states have a nice fucking picture of him."

"If he hasn't already altered his appearance," Brian pointed out.

"Or if he's not long gone by now." Craig thrust his hands into his pockets.

"Let's hope he still intends to go after Longnecker." Brian hastened his pace as he headed farther up the street. "Craig, will you let me check out the hit and run scene?"

"I don't see why not." Craig escorted Brian past several patrol officers and pointed to where the dark skid marks started on the pavement. Several citizens were standing along the sidewalk, watching the events unfold. Among them was a shabbily dressed old man with long straggly hair. He was holding a tarnished cane. His attention was primarily focused on Brian Jeffers. He inched closer to the yellow barrier tape. A patrol officer reached out and stopped his progress.

"You have to stay behind the tape. Do you understand?"

"I'm sorry. I didn't mean to get too close."

The officer smiled. "Trying to keep everybody safe, Sir."

The elderly man pointed in the direction of Brian Jeffers and said, "I know that man. Is he in charge here?"

The officer glanced over. "That's Detective Berte. Did you see something, Sir?"

"Not that man. The other one." He pointed his cane in the direction of Brian Jeffers.

"I don't know who he is. Did you see something, Sir?" the officer asked again.

"No. He just reminds me of someone I used to know. Sir, I'm sorry to cause trouble. I will be on my way now."

The patrol officer looked annoyed. "Fine."

The elderly man pushed through several onlookers and then hobbled around the block and went back to the scene so that he could look at the former detective of Valentine one more time. *So Ronald didn't kill you.* He waved at a few patrol cars as he passed by. *Right under your noses. My disguise worked and, best of all, Brian Jeffers is alive, which means I can go after my fifty-cent piece. That's why he is here—to try and catch me before I kill Samuel.* Lucas wasn't about to let that happen, but it excited him to think Jeffers still had the coin with him. He reached into his tattered pants pocket and tightly gripped the necklace. *Tomorrow, Samuel will be waking up for the last time. It has been a long time in the making, but I will finally have my day of vengeance.*

# Chapter 43

# Imminent Attack

Samuel Longnecker peered out into the softly lit auditorium as he finished the last line of his speech. No applause followed. It was silent, except for the sound of the building's boiler emanating through the large heating vents. *Doesn't sound too bad.* He enjoyed rehearsing in front of an empty audience. It was part of a routine he had started years before.

Samuel picked up a glass from the second shelf of the podium and took a sip of the ageless brandy. He sloshed it around in his mouth, taking in the wonderful aroma before he swallowed. He had been thinking about what the female detective had said about being on Lucas Calling's target list. *Lucas would be a fool to come after me in a public place.* Samuel had spotted the undercover officers in the hotel. One even sat across from him at a local restaurant. *If he wants to kill me, he will have to go through them first. What happened to Lucas was a true tragedy, but I'm not going to shoulder all the blame.*

Samuel poured himself another drink. The creaking sound of a door being opened caused him to drop the bottle of liquor. It shattered on the tile floor.

Samuel instinctively bent down to pick up the shards of glass.

"Shit. Anybody there?" Samuel called out.

Heavy footsteps approached him from behind.

Samuel whirled around, holding a piece of glass in an offensive manner.

"Whoa, what are you doing?" Wallace Meredith asked as he stood there with his arms raised.

Samuel dropped the glass shard onto the ground. "Wallace, sorry, thought you were somebody else."

"Who?" Wallace asked with a worried look.

Samuel waved him off. "Uh, no one . . . just got the jitters."

"Something obviously scared the wits out of you. What's going on Samuel?" Wallace cocked his head, expecting an answer.

"Have you heard anything about the recent murders in town?" Samuel asked.

"Not really. Why do you ask?" Wallace put a hand on the distraught physician's shoulder.

"A couple of detectives came to see me yesterday. They mentioned some murders with Propaganician being involved."

Wallace turned pale. "Propaganician is your creation."

"Not just mine. Do you remember a Dr. Lucas Calling?"

Wallace had a blank expression on his face. "No, I don't remember anyone by that name."

"I forgot. You didn't start working there until after he was fired."

"This Dr. Calling was fired?"

"Yes, he was my protégé . . . and partner."

"So the police think he used the Propaganician?"

"More to it than that. They showed me pictures."

"Pictures of the victims?"

"Wallace, they were slaughtered and the bodies were torn apart."

"So this Lucas person is now coming after you?"

"The police seem to think so. They think so enough that they put a detail on me for extra protection."

Wallace looked concerned. "I didn't see anybody out there when I came in."

Samuel shrugged. "Probably trying to stay hidden until they are actually needed."

"Seriously, if you want to cancel the engagement, I will understand."

"I'm not going to do that to you. It was a cost for you to bring me here," Samuel said with a small grin.

"Money means nothing. Your safety concerns are—"

"—It's only one more night. Besides, the police do have someone watching me." Samuel tapped his knuckles against the wood.

"Well, if you say so, but make sure to lock the door next time." Wallace pointed to the back door.

"Most definitely." Samuel glanced at his watch. "I will see you here at seven sharp."

Wallace Meredith left the building while Samuel cleaned up the mess on the stage. *Can I really cancel and get out of here? No, that wouldn't be fair to everyone.* He picked up his notes and resumed his speech, starting from the beginning. *In a few hours, I will give my presentation and then check out of the hotel, leaving Lucas Calling far behind—hopefully forever.*

Lucas edged along the tree line, making sure to stay out of sight. The heavyset undercover officer behind the steering wheel seemed to be engrossed in the local newspaper. He didn't even turn around when Lucas chucked a snowball on top of the car hood. The man only looked up once in the hour long period that Lucas had been watching him, and the only reason he even looked up once was because a couple of pretty girls were involved in a sexy snowball fight. *Not even a challenge.* Lucas glanced down at his left leg to check the surgical tape. *Good and tight.* He dropped to his hands and knees and slowly crawled down the hill. Darkness had made the ground even colder. The snow was quick to penetrate his polyester disguise. He knew the combination of decorated pine trees and ice sculptures would hide him until he was at the set of dumpsters. The dumpsters were several hundred feet from where the unmarked car was parked, which would give Lucas considerable time to act if the undercover officer did see him.

Lucas removed the semi-automatic from his hip holster and screwed the sound suppressor on the end of the barrel, being careful not to make any noise that would give him away. Then he tucked the gun into the front waistband of his pants and covered it with his jacket. He scooted to the back of a large dumpster and cautiously rose to his feet. He reached down along his left leg and ripped the white tape away. The cane slid into his hands. He scoured the wooden stick for any tape residue. *Even the slightest error could give me away.* When he was satisfied everything was just right, he hobbled out from behind the garbage and headed toward the blue sedan.

The undercover officer was still reading the paper when Lucas appeared in his rearview mirror. Lucas knocked on the rear window, startling him. The heavyset man flung open the door. He was irritated.

"What are you doing?" the undercover officer demanded to know.

Lucas smiled. "I'm sorry. I didn't mean to startle you, but I need some assistance."

The undercover officer had his hand under his coat. "Okay, what's so important?"

Lucas hobbled closer. "I think there was a murder. You are the police, aren't you?"

The undercover officer looked even more enraged. "A murder! What are talking about, old man?"

"The man on television. He's in the hotel," Lucas said.

"How do you know that?"

"He killed a woman. I saw him by the dumpsters over there." Lucas pointed his cane at the two dumpsters.

The undercover officer glared over at the garbage. "Over there? Okay, show me."

"The body is in the garbage, Sir."

Lucas escorted the officer to the garbage cans.

"Which can?" The undercover officer reached into his coat.

"The first one. Sorry, I meant the one on the right."

The undercover officer rushed by Lucas and lifted the lid off the can.

Lucas pulled the semi-automatic out of his waistband and aimed it at the back of the undercover officer's head. "Do you see it, Sir?"

"What the fuck is wrong with you? Are you some kind of nut? There is nothing here!"

"Yes there is." Lucas squeezed the trigger. The bullet caught the undercover officer in the back of the head, splattering his inner thought processes on the front of the trash receptacle. A small item dropped from his waist as he slumped to the ground. Lucas smiled as he watched the man's body shake in violent spasms and then abruptly freeze, becoming completely still.

Lucas scanned the area to make sure no one witnessed the shooting. Convinced that there were no witnesses, he stepped over the body and lifted the lid off the dumpster. Then he picked up the man and catapulted him into the opening. He looked inside of the dumpster to get one last look at the body and then flipped the lid closed.

Something on the ground caught Lucas' attention. It was the item that had fallen from the undercover officer's waist. Lucas bent down and picked it up. It was a mini portable radio. *Now I will know where everyone is.* He clipped it to his belt and laughed out loud.

Lucas hurried back to the unmarked car and opened the door. *Still in the ignition.* He got in the car. As he drove away from the hotel, he listened to the various chatter coming from the police radio. One of the things he heard was that Samuel was still at the venue for the performance that night. More than likely, the remaining member of the security detail would be the only one accompanying him. *If the second bodyguard is anything like the first, this will be almost comical.* Lucas felt the years of hate surging through his body as he got closer to fulfilling his collection.

# Chapter 44

# Deadly and Demented

Brian Jeffers was at the vending machines in the emergency room, scouring the rows of plastic wrapped carbohydrates when Craig patted him on the shoulder.

"Hey, you have been here since early this morning. Why don't you go to the hotel and get some sleep."

Brian turned to face him. "Not a chance. She was trying to help me out. I owe this much to her."

Brian and Craig had spent the entire previous night in search of any witnesses who might have seen the vicious rundown of Kelli Jordan. The two weary men arrived at Marcona General right as the sun was coming up. There was no change in her condition. Craig went to work, but Brian stayed at the hospital. Brian had waited throughout the entire day and into the night.

"Then, you're gonna need this." Craig handed him a cup of coffee and smiled.

"Thanks. I was beginning to feel like a zombie. Did you get a chance to talk to the doc?"

"She's still in surgery," Craig said.

"Seems very strong-willed," Brian said, sounding hopeful.

"You don't know the half of it. That girl is tougher than most guys I know," Craig said in a matter of fact voice.

"I bet. Does she have any family? I didn't see anyone in the waiting room."

"Not anymore. Her mother and father died when she was young. Raised by her grandmother, but she passed away after Kelli graduated college."

"Sounds like a hard life."

"Fucking too hard. Now this!"

Brian was dizzy. The pain in his chest was really bad. The lack of much needed sleep was beginning to take its toll.

"I need to sit down for a minute."

"Shit, you look like you need a doctor, too. Want me to call a nurse?"

Brian glared at Craig. "No, I don't want a nurse. Just a minute to sit down."

Brian turned around and saw a metal chair next to an orange cafeteria table. He walked over to it, pulled it out from the table, and sat down.

Craig walked up to Brian. He bent down next to him and asked, "Are you all right?"

Brian waved him off.

A green flyer on the table caught Brian's attention. It was propped up against a napkin holder. Brian grabbed the flyer and read what it said. Shit! He stood up so quickly that he lost his balance.

Craig caught Brian, preventing him from falling to the ground. "What are you doing? I thought you needed to relax."

Brian thrust the flyer at Craig. "Look at this. The event is tonight." Brian peeked down at his digital watch. "Shit. Just two hours away."

Craig grabbed the flyer. "Brian, it's cool. Kelli put two undercovers on him. This Lucas asshole—he won't be able to get by both of them."

Brian almost ran past Craig. "Lucas has been stalking him. You can count on it. Don't you think he knows about the bodyguards?"

Craig shook his head. "Even if he does, the fucker's picture is everywhere. He won't even be able to get close to this Longnecker guy."

Brian felt dizzy. He bolted through the emergency room door and headed for his car. He knew the madman wouldn't care if his photo was being spread around like wildfire. He would just find a way to work around the inconvenience.

Brian opened the glove box and removed the brown paper bag. Then he turned on the engine. Craig Berte emerged from the hospital and stared at Brian. Brian ignored Craig's look of disbelief as he shot out into the roadway, praying he wasn't too late.

Lucas parked the sedan in a vacant spot on the west side of the auditorium. The portable radio on his belt buzzed to life.

"SA-1 to SA-2, you copy?"

Lucas didn't say anything. He wanted to see if the radio transmission would be repeated.

"SA-1 to SA-2, you copying my radio traffic?"

Lucas thought about what that call sign might mean. He smiled. *Oh, special assignment, of course. Why doesn't that surprise me?*

Lucas pushed the button on the microphone and said "SA-2 to SA-1?"

"SA-2, you sound a little different. Must be these portables. Everything good to go?"

Lucas remembered hearing some radio protocol in the past and felt comfortable enough to use standard lingo. "10-4. Just a little problem with the radio."

The portable squelched. "10-4. Be advised, our subject looks like he is done rehearsing."

Lucas smiled. "What's your location?"

"In my car. Parking lot, east side of the auditorium. I'm next to where the subject parked his vehicle. You still at the hotel?"

Lucas hesitated for a moment. "10-4. Until I hear anything else, I will be here."

"I think this guy's speech starts in about an hour and a half. You copy?"

"10-4. Does he know you're in the lot?" Lucas asked. He pulled away from the parking spot adjacent to the building. "Possibly, but who knows? This is a clandestine assignment," the man joked.

"SA-1, have you taken a dinner break yet?" Lucas laughed after he released the button.

"I was going to call one in after this guy started his speech, since you will be covering the event."

"SA-1, I will head that way and radio you once I get close.

Don't worry. I will take care of everything." *Of course I will take care of everything.*

"10-4, SA-2. I appreciate it. This individual will be leaving town tomorrow, and then he will be somebody else's problem."

*He's leaving sooner than that.* "10-4. I'm leaving the hotel now. Should be there within ten minutes."

Lucas slowly drove along the backside of the auditorium. A few of the event security were just arriving. He glanced at his watch. *Close enough to ten minutes.* He drove to the east parking lot and turned in. A duplicate sedan of the one he was driving was parked in the lot next to the auditorium's botanical garden. He looked at the plant life. *Hmm, that is different,* he thought. The botanical garden didn't house the typical plants found in those types of places. Instead, there were several evergreen trees of various sizes, all adorned with Christmas decorations. He pulled closer to the duplicate sedan and flashed his high beams at the undercover officer.

The portable crackled. "SA-2, thanks. Have a peaceful tour. I will meet you back at the hotel when you're done."

*No, you won't.* "10-4. See ya then."

The duplicate sedan pulled out of the parking lot.

Lucas surveyed the area. He spotted Samuel's snow covered rental car, but nothing else caught his attention. *Nobody is here to get in my way.* Lucas stepped out of the car, stripped off his first layer of clothes, and peeled off the hairpiece. He adjusted his belt and patted down the pockets of his cargo pants to make sure the knife was still securely in place. *Perfect.* He pulled a dark garbage bag out of his left cargo pocket and stuffed everything into it. Then he tied the plastic in a knot and threw the bag in the car. Ready for his plan, he trudged off to hide among the evergreens.

Lucas had been so busy getting everything prepared that hadn't realized it was snowing until he was standing still behind the evergreen trees. The snow was getting heavier by the minute. He stood behind the trees for quite some time before he saw his mentor walk out of the arena. Samuel looked out into the lot and scanned the area for unseen threats as he hurried to his car.

Lucas had a death grip on the blade as he watched his target brush away the snow from the windows of the sedan. He had waited in anticipation for Samuel Longnecker since moving to the area. Lucas had missed his chance with Samuel two months earlier because the esteemed physician canceled his engagement at the Palladium in Dementia. Finally, Lucas was fulfilling his masterpiece. *Too long to wait for vengeance.*

Lucas readied the blade. He had to admit, the botanical garden was a perfect place to conceal himself. *I'm sure the architects never had this in mind.* Lucas reached into his cargo pocket with his free hand and removed a small syringe of the paralytic concoction that he and Samuel had perfected years earlier. *A fitting end for you, dear friend.*

Samuel cleared off the remaining patch of snow and ice from the rear windshield and was doing his best to force open the frozen driver's side door when he heard a voice call out.

"Help me! Help me, someone!" Samuel faced the direction of the voice. "Who's there? Are you oka—y? Do you need me to call the police? They are over in the sedan, right over there." He pointed in the direction of the undercover patrol car Lucas had been driving.

Samuel's hands started to shake. The cold air was pressing against his vocal cords. He slowly approached the trees, wondering if someone needed his help or if they were pulling a practical joke on him. He reached out as he moved through the maze of foliage. He was getting colder by the minute, but he did hear a cry for help, and it would look inappropriate if he abandoned someone who was actually injured.

"Hello. If you can hear my voice, say something. My name is Samuel. I'm a doctor."

Lucas heard Samuel's voice get louder as he came closer. *Just a few more steps and I will have you.* Lucas smiled. The tree in front of him started to move. Large chunks of snow fell from its branches. Lucas steadied the blade and waited for Samuel. He would be there within seconds. *Goodbye, Samuel.* The branches of the tree stopped moving, and Lucas didn't hear Samuel's voice any longer. *Where did he go?* His heart started beating faster and his composure began slipping away. *Something is not right.* Lucas' adrenalin levels were off the charts as he moved forward to find Samuel. His usual smoothness and precision of approaching his prey had been replaced with overeagerness, and by his normal standards, he was just short of reckless abandon.

Lucas broke through the branches—an action that proved to be a mistake of substantial proportions.

Someone slipped in behind Lucas, and there was nothing he could do about it. He tried to rectify his miscalculation, but he knew it was a futile effort. He whirled around, swinging the blade, trying to inflict his aggressor with as much pain as possible. Brian Jeffers surprised Lucas with 200,000 volts of white-hot electricity. The steel prongs dug into Lucas' chest, causing him to stagger back, dazed and in pain. Lucas tried to regroup and ward off Brian, but he failed miserably. Brian zapped him again. The prongs went deep into the fleshy part of his thigh.

"Ahhh," Lucas cried out in anguish as he collapsed to the ground.

Brian withdrew the weapon and took a step backward to assess the killer.

Lucas tried to stand up, but his legs were shaking too much.

"No, you bastard, you're not getting away this time."

Brian rushed at Lucas and thrust the weapon into his throat. The zap caused Lucas to drop his knife and syringe. Lucas stretched out his arms, scrambling to reach the plastic tube, but again, Brian was right there. He shoved the stun gun into Lucas' mouth, splitting his lips in two, breaking several of the madman's teeth. Lucas looked up. Tears of pain cascaded down his face. Brian pushed the switch on the weapon. Wave after wave of electric justice pierced through Lucas' skull. Brian wasn't sure how long he had held the button down, but it was long enough because when he removed the stun gun, he could smell a strong odor of burning flesh. Small puffs of steam were coming from Lucas' mouth.

Brian tucked the weapon into his waistband and covered it with his jacket. He glared down at Dr. Lucas Calling and knew the man was still alive. He bent down to search the ground for one of the items Lucas had dropped. *There it is.* Brian picked up the syringe. He knelt down beside the killer of his wife and child. He started to shake as he gripped the needle with both hands and raised it above his head. Brian Jeffers then plunged the tube of Propaganician deep into the heart of Lucas Calling. Lucas convulsed, and then he died.

The neck chain Lucas was wearing had been hidden by his shirt. During the fight, it had slipped out into view. Brian caught a glimpse of the jewelry and leaned in closer. I've seen that before. Brian suddenly recognized the heart-shaped pendant. He reached over and ripped it from the dead man's throat. *This belonged to Melissa.* Brian opened the pendant and smiled. A picture of his daughter was on one side of the glass inlay. The other side had something quite unexpected. It was a picture of Brian Jeffers in his uniform, shortly after graduating from the police academy. Brian stood up and put the necklace inside his shirt pocket. He glanced at Lucas as he reached into his front pants pocket and pulled out something familiar to the killer. He flicked it on the icy surface. The fifty-cent coin rolled until it found a home next to the dead man.

Brian Jeffers walked out from the mass of decorated trees, and looked up at the night sky. The North Star could be seen with clarity, and Brian rejoiced as he gazed upon its sparkling beauty. Brian headed back to his car with a feeling of renewed spirit and peace, which was something he hadn't felt in a long time.

# Epilogue

Brian stepped off the elevator and headed in the direction of Kelli Jordan's hospital room. He wasn't sure if Kelli liked yellow roses, but it was all he could think of. He turned the corner and noticed Craig Berte was standing outside the door waiting for him.

"Hey, I wanted to let you know, our guy killed someone else. We just found out about it. She was someone at that hotel Samuel Longnecker was staying at."

"Who was it?" Brian asked.

"A woman in the room next door to him. Felicity Holt was her name."

"How did she die?"

"He used that drug, but he also drenched her with some wine to make it look like she had alcohol poisoning."

*Another victim. At least there won't be any more.* "Sorry we didn't get to her in time," Brian said. He shook his head in sorrow.

"So am I." Craig gawked at the flowers. "Brian, that's not all. I wanted to apologize for everything."

Brian shook his head and extended his hand. "Forget it.

The important thing is your partner is alive . . . and Lucas is gone for good."

Craig straightened his tie. "There is one more thing we need to discuss."

*Here it comes,* Brian thought. "Sure, what's up?"

"Lucas Calling's body had several burns on the face, chest, and leg areas. Any chance you know how he got those? Craig asked. He folded his arms across his chest.

Brian had a blank expression. "No idea at all. Anything else you need to know?"

Craig smiled. "How did the syringe end up in his chest, Brian?"

Brian shrugged. "Like I told your boss, we struggled, and the guy tried to stab me with it. He ended up getting it instead."

Craig winked. "That's good enough for me. I just wanted to make sure I covered everything in the report."

*Really, that was it?* Brian was surprised.

"Can never be too thorough. Well, now that I'm done with my investigation, I will let you go see Kelli. Oh, Brian, I'm glad you're all right." Craig smiled and walked away without waiting for Brian to say anything.

Brian tapped on Kelli Jordan's door.

"Come in," Kelli said in a faint voice.

Brian walked in, stopped at the foot of her bed, and waved the flowers at her. "For you. I wasn't sure if you liked flowers or not, but I figured it couldn't hurt."

Kelli smiled. She had several stitches on her face, and her body was bandaged in several places, but she was alive. "I'm a girl. Of course I like flowers," she said. Then she motioned for him to move closer to her.

"Well, I guess we get to finally meet." Brian chuckled. He placed the roses on the table next to her.

"Thanks for getting him." Kelli reached out to touch Brian on the arm.

Brian placed his hand on hers. "We did it together. If you hadn't gotten in contact with me, Lucas would still be out there."

Kelli nodded. "We could almost be partners."

Brian sat down in the chair next to Kelli's bed. He looked at her and thought, *She is very intriguing and strong. Even though her face is scarred, she is sensual and alluring.*

"I think, in a sense, we're already partners," Brian said. He reached over to the table and poured her a cup of water.

Kelli stared at him. "So what's next for you?"

Brian took a deep breath. "Going to get my daughters and am going to finally go home."

"So back to the chief of police duties then, I take it?" Kelli asked.

Brian hesitated for a bit before answering. "I don't think so," he finally said, "I still have this pain in my chest, so I might just take some time off."

"I was thinking the same thing. I'm going to be off work a while myself, and I do remember someone saying he was going to make me a nice dinner."

"That's right. I do still owe you that. Technically, though, I never spent the night at your house," Brian joked.

"That can be arranged." Kelli blushed like a high school girl.

Brian felt a strong connection to Kelli. It seemed like she

had the same feelings for him. Maybe it was because they both had been damaged in a way that would make most people give up on living, or maybe hurting souls have a way of finding each other. Whatever the reason was, Brian Jeffers would be foolish if he didn't explore their newfound friendship and find out where it would lead them.

The end.

Milton Keynes UK
Ingram Content Group UK Ltd.
UKHW010159061223
433783UK00003B/156